"YOU MUST NEV
MARRY AN ENG
Princess Ida said.

Princess Adelaide listened to her sister, but said nothing.

"They are the most evil and lecherous throughout Europe," Ida went on. "Their father is a madman, locked away in a padded room. And it is said that when the mad king dies, there will be a revolution, and every noble head in the kingdom will roll."

Again Adelaide said nothing.

But the day came when Prince William, son of the "mad king" and father of ten illegitimate children, asked her if she would become his wife, and perhaps the next Queen of England.

A sister's advice is no match for the demands of the heart. "Yes, I will," said Princess Adelaide.

A BOUQUET OF BRIDES
was originally published by
Hurst & Blackett Ltd.

Books by Rose Meadows

*A Bouquet of Brides
*Farewell to Love (Original British title: The Show Must Go On)
 The Imperial Pawn
*The Queen's Consent
* Royal Mistress
 To Be My Wedded Wife

*Published by POCKET BOOKS

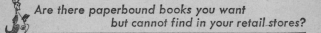

ROSE MEADOWS

A Bouquet of Brides

PUBLISHED BY POCKET BOOKS NEW YORK

A BOUQUET OF BRIDES

Hurst & Blackett edition published 1970

POCKET BOOK edition published March, 1974

L

This POCKET BOOK edition includes every word contained
in the original, higher-priced edition. It is printed from
brand-new plates made from completely reset, clear, easy-to-
read type. POCKET BOOK editions are published by POCKET
BOOKS, a division of Simon & Schuster, Inc., 630 Fifth
Avenue, New York, N.Y. 10020. Trademarks registered
in the United States and other countries.

Standard Book Number: 671-77717-3.
Cover illustration by Betty Maxey.

Printed in the U.S.A.

A Bouquet of Brides

Prologue

I

The straggling column of bedraggled men slowly wound its way through the outskirts of London, cursing violently as the torrential rain soaked through their tattered rags. Hungry and footsore they might be, but the leaders repeatedly shouted encouragement to their more weary companions, that they had at least arrived in time . . . in time to join in the royal wedding celebrations . . . to create all the mischief that angry, hungry men could conceive . . . anything to show these flaunting royal princes, and the haughty arrogant aristocracy, that they were nearing the end of their endurance.

For some of them, this was not their first protest march, and now they were arguing among themselves as to the right direction for Tottenham Court Road, where assuredly they could find shelter for the night, provided they were not too particular about sharing the crowded floors with a motley collection of unwashed bodies.

As they pointed out the saturated banners and bunting hanging from windows and stretched across the streets, now looking drab and washed out, their brilliant blues and scarlets having intermingled into dull funereal shades, they guffawed with laughter. Perhaps the rain was to their advantage after all. It would be an extra cause for jeers to see all the fine ladies getting a soaking as they stepped from their carriages to go mincing over the cobbles and puddles to their places on the stands . . . all just to crane their necks to get a good view of Princess Charlotte and her bridegroom, Prince Leopold of Coburg.

Damnation and Hell to all these Germans, both male

and female who kept coming over to England . . . coming here to be housed and fed and given vast incomes. They spat vigorously at the mention of all the money that was being lavished just to legalize a princess bedding with a prince. Coarse and lewd jokes about the young couple were tossed from one to another; the only way they could raise a laugh, as they trudged along.

They had already arranged their allotted tasks for the morrow, mixing with the crowds, shouting insults, stirring up arguments and joining in brawls and fights. With any sharp instrument they might possess, they would stab and prick the cavalry horses lining the route of the royal procession, gloating when they reared in pain and threw their scarlet-uniformed mounts. Others would be strewing the roads with nails and rubble all in the hope of laming the horses and upsetting the carriages.

Of course there was the risk of being killed themselves, if they were charged by the militia, but in their present desperate state of wretchedness, that was of little importance. Surely now that the nineteenth century was well on its way, some thought should be given to the betterment of the workers.

God! How it made them want to retch at the thought of the food that would be wasted at the wedding banquets, while their women and children left behind, scarce knew the meaning of a satisfied stomach.

Oh, yes, the parish councils were preening themselves on the celebrations they were providing for the bairns; a few sweetmeats, a confection or two, and perhaps a meat pie . . . not forgetting the new ribbons for the maypole, round which they would dance . . . at least those who had the encrgy to do so.

Not that the councils had fallen willingly into line. Where was the money to come from? They needed all their scanty funds for the increasing number of destitute, but the high and mighty, dictating from their country seats and town houses, had stressed that they must put on a show to woo back the grumbling, restless workers.

The factory owners, to show their magnanimity, had decreed a general day's holiday . . . without pay of course, which only incensed the smouldering unrest. Their pay of fifteen shillings a week, for a fourteen-hour day, was meager enough when a small loaf of bread cost one and nine. Their leaders had urged for higher wages; the unemployed had smashed up machinery that had taken away their jobs, and now from the various northern towns, the protesting marchers were converging on the capital.

It was still raining when they emerged from their shelter the following morning, yawning and scratching themselves, glad to gulp in the fresh air, after sharing the stuffiness of an unventilated hovel with about twenty others. The immediate question was how to get some food without money. Their hosts were willing to help. Go down to the fashionable parts of Piccadilly and Oxford Street, they told them; push and shove; hustle and bustle, and pick a few pockets . . . then the gin shops and the trays of the piemen would be at their command.

But why, in the name of God, could the marriage not take place before nine o'clock in the evening? Both leaders and followers alike instinctively felt that, long before then, their hunger and their soaked skins would so dampen their spirits, that their protests would fizzle out like damp squibs.

Why, oh why, had the wedding ceremony been arranged for so late in the evening? As Princess Charlotte, sat motionless, posing for Mr. Turnerelli, the sculptor, the question repeatedly rose up in her mind. Yet she was glad of this respite, to sit quietly, away from the everlasting fussing of Aunt Mary and Aunt Augusta.

She could hardly believe in her good fortune; that her marriage was not an arranged affair, but one of true, mutual love. Strange too, that when they met that first time, eighteen months ago, she had almost ignored him, being so bedeviled as how to break off her engagement with William of Orange and persuade Papa to allow her to marry her nineteen-year-old cousin Prince Frederick of Prussia whom she loved to such distraction. No, that had not been love, as she soon discovered, when Frederick's passionate letters from Berlin became cooler and shorter, terminating with the return of her portrait, which she had given him to gaze upon, until their next meeting.

For weeks she had wept and pined; not so much for the loss of a bridegroom, but for the receding chance of having an establishment of her own. Then she had recalled that afternoon at Pulteney's Hotel, where she had gone to call upon the Tsar's sister, the Grand Duchess of Oldenburg; recalled the young man she had met upon that back staircase, who had introduced himself as Prince Leopold of Saxe-Coburg and had so courteously escorted her to her waiting carriage.

What had he been doing in England? More to the point, why had he been on that back staircase, used by her, to ensure privacy?

Making cautious inquiries, she learned that he had actually approached the Regent for her hand in marriage, only to be so violently repulsed, that he had been glad to return to Saxe-Coburg. It all seemed so hopeless, until dear Uncle Frederick, Duke of York, had come to the rescue, persuading her father to write to Leopold, belatedly inviting him to England to discuss the possibility of the match.

Leopold had been in England now for two months; two months of getting to know each other; of falling in love more and more, as each day sped happily by, all converging on this day . . . their wedding day.

He was so understanding; so tolerant of her many failings; so sympathetic about poor Mama. She had, with her customary bluntness, quizzed him as to his knowledge.

"You have heard of my mother's . . . her misdemeanors . . . ?"

"I have, Princess."

His voice was so quiet, so ordinary, that she had looked at him in surprise.

"Yet you do not hold it against me . . . and our marriage?"

"Why should I?" Again the quiet level voice.

"Then what is your opinion of her? Do not mince your words, Sir, for whatever you say, I shall still tell you that I love her."

"I am indeed glad of that, Princess. To have said anything different would have surprised me. I am marrying into your family, Princess, and from now onwards, I owe your parents loyalty and respect."

"Knowing what you know . . ."

"Whatever I think of their past behavior, I keep to myself. It is their future actions . . . actions that might hurt or grieve you, to which I, as your husband, shall take exception." Dear, dear Leopold, so wise and sensible. She could only shake her head and whisper, *"My mother was bad but she would not have become so bad if my father had not been infinitely worse."*

He had taken her hand, pressed it between his and then had bent and kissed it.

A smile of contented happiness lit up her face causing Mr. Turnerelli to look more keenly at his royal sitter. The Princess was more beautiful than he had ever imagined her.

She was recalling the day when she and the Prince had gone to look over *Claremont Park,* built for Lord Clive of India and now at a cost of £66,000, bought by the government as the country's wedding gift to the future queen and her consort.

The well-laid-out grounds, the work of Capability Brown, had entranced them, but when, hand in hand, they had walked up the wide stone steps and entered the oval black and white hall, then excitedly ran from room to room, each opening from the other, they knew that no other house could be so beautiful.

The Prince had peremptorily ordered her ladies to wait below while they went to inspect the upper floor. She had been amused at the shocked looks on their faces, knowing that the Queen's orders were that they were not to be let out of their sight, and once out of earshot, she could not resist sharing the joke with Leopold.

For reply, he had taken her gently in his arms and kissed her full on the lips, their first real kiss of love; not one of pent-up passion just released, but rather of controlled, deep abiding love. In that moment she had known that her love for him was returned with equal fervor.

"I've been longing to do that for a long time, Charlotte, my *liebchen,* but it was too precious to make it a public exhibition . . ."

All the way home they had chattered about the furniture they would buy with the £40,000 allowance . . . how they would expend their £60,000 annual income . . . the jewels she could buy for £10,000 and the dresses . . .

The tall, elegant young man, neatly dressed in blue jacket, buff waistcoat and grey pantaloons, stepped through the french window, out on to the balcony of *Clarence House.* Immediately, there was an uproar of huzzas, shouts and wild cheering. He had lost count of how many appearances he had already made that morning, but each time he attempted a final wave, there were cries of, "Don't go in yet, Leo!" "Isn't he a bonny lad?" "Drop of English rain won't hurt you, Mister Coburg." The English rain had hurt him, developing rheumatic fever almost as soon as he arrived. Now Dr. Stockmar, his physician, was forever warning him, but this morning, neither Stockmar nor anyone else could dictate to him.

As he looked out at the sea of faces, he could hardly credit his good fortune; that these English folk, reputedly undemonstrative and cold should be so enthusiastic about this marriage . . . that until now, his yearly income had been but £200. More unbelievable still, that his bride should be Princess Charlotte, some day to be Queen of England and he her consort. True, the Tsar's sister had tried to engineer the match eighteen months ago, instructing him to come to England immediately and call on her at the Pulteney Hotel, where she would arrange for the Princess to be there at the same time. They had met, but something went wrong; the meeting fell flat. A haughty madam, he had told himself. Willful and obstinate too, for only a few days later he had heard of the broken engagement between her and William of Orange.

But she was neither willful nor obstinate. She was

adorable; gay, laughter loving, yet capable of responding to his quieter mood. Oh yes, his dear little Charlotte could be coaxed and led! Why, when he had laughingly remonstrated about her constant fidgeting when talking, and of stamping her feet to emphasize a point, she had instantly expressed her firm intention to eradicate both annoyances. What was it his future father-in-law had said last night? *"If you don't resist, she will govern you with a high hand."* He had no fear for their future happiness. He was going to give to Charlotte that which her parents had denied her . . . love and affection.

The hand of the small french clock was creeping up to nine. Charlotte gazed at her reflection. The diamonds at her throat and in her ears glittered with such brilliancy that they lit up the mirror. A chuckle of irrepressible excitement escaped her, causing Aunt Mary to look at her with alarm.

"Are you all right, child?"

"Of course, Aunt. It was just that I couldn't see my face for the gleam of diamonds."

"Well, here are more . . . your tiara. Let me fix it for you."

Atop the fair, naturally wavy hair, Princess Mary skillfully fixed the diamond circlet.

"There, now you are ready. Stand up, child, and let me have a good look at you." Charlotte, however, continued to stare in the mirror and then suddenly, without turning, asked in a low voice:

"What was Mama's wedding dress like? Did she wear diamonds?"

She heard her aunt's gasp of indrawn breath.

"Why, Charlotte, what a time to ask such a question!"

"What better time, Aunt Mary, than on my wedding day . . . thinking about her . . . wishing that she were here . . . ?"

"That is dangerous talk, child. What would your father say . . . what would the Prince think . . . ?"

"He knows what I think . . ."

"You mean you have spoken to him about her . . . ?"

"And why not? When we are settled in *Claremont,* I shall invite her to stay . . . Married . . . I shall no longer be under my father's domination."

She rose, smiling without any sign of emotion or agitation. Her gown of silver lamé and net over a tissue slip, had a broad hem of silver embroidery and Brussels lace, while the silver train, lined with white satin, fastened at the front with a diamond clasp. Mrs. Triaud of Bond Street had really excelled herself.

With her aunt on one side and a colonel on the other, Charlotte walked slowly down the broad staircase of the Queen's House and then, along with her grandmother, the Queen, who now joined them, entered the bridal carriage to take them to *Carlton House.*

As the crowd's uproarious welcome shattered the spring night, Charlotte beamed impishly at her grandmother. *"Bless me, what a crowd."*

All the way to *Carlton House,* she was accompanied by tumultuous cheering; then she was walking up the steps of her father's house . . . along the richly carpeted corridors towards the Great Crimson Room, where candles, six feet high, blazed away in huge crystal chandeliers suspended from the ceiling . . . where her father and all her uncles and aunts awaited her . . . and Leopold . . . her beloved Leopold.

He turned slightly at her entrance, to greet her with a loving smile, and as their eyes met, she felt her heart would burst with love and pride. How handsome he looked in his uniform of a British general . . . the scarlet tunic . . . the white Kerseymere waistcoat and breeches. What other prince could display so many emblems of knighthood conferred for valor?

Almost in a dream, she found herself standing by his side; her father nearby; gross and obese in his field marshal's uniform; yet for once smiling benignly, despite the pain of his gouty legs.

She roused herself, to repeat her vows in a loud, clear voice. Humbly she knelt on the crimson velvet cushion to receive the blessing . . . to pray . . . to pray that her happiness should go on . . . and on . . .

Now she was Princess Charlotte of Saxe-Coburg. The guns from the Tower of London and St. James's Park roared out a royal salute, the signal for all the church bells of London to burst into a joyous peal.

How much longer before they could leave *Carlton House?* There were the toasts to be proposed . . . to drink . . . and more toasts. Everyone wanted to talk to her . . . dear Uncle William, with messages of love from George Fitzclarence and his other children . . . Uncle Frederick and his duchess, who were lending them their country house, *Oatlands,* for the honeymoon, but at last, she was free to escape and change into her going-away clothes.

Her governess, Mrs. Campbell, helped her, tears running down her cheeks. "You look so beautiful, Your Highness . . . so happy."

"I am certainly a most fortunate creature and have to bless God. A princess, never, I believe, set out in life or married with such prospects of happiness . . . real domestic ones like other people . . ."

The Queen came shuffling in, critically eyeing the bride in her white satin-ermine-trimmed pelisse. As Mrs. Campbell fixed Charlotte's hat, a creation of white satin, lace and ostrich feathers, Her Majesty remarked, "You, Mrs. Campbell, will of course be traveling in the same coach as the Prince and Princess."

"Why no, Your Majesty . . ."

"But it will be so immodest to allow them to travel alone."

"Your Majesty, I regret to differ, but they are now man and wife . . ."

Between pinches of snuff, the old lady muttered inaudibly and shuffled out of the room. Charlotte turned and hugged Mrs. Campbell. "Oh, thank you. Thank you . . . and don't let her bully you into joining us at *Oatlands,* will you? We do so want to be alone."

Now they were in the coach, the six beautiful greys, each sporting its white satin rosette, nervously straining on the reins, anxious to get away from all the noise and tumult. At last they were clattering down the Mall, the outriders driving back the crowds to clear the roadway. All along the route, they were accompanied by vociferous cheering reaching a still higher crescendo whenever the street oil lamps outlined the newly-weds, sitting so closely together.

At last they were out in the country, leaving London and its noisy drunken rabble behind, changing to the warm greeting of the villagers; bonfires flashing the good news from hamlet to hamlet.

An air of wondrous peace and solemnity seemed to fill the coach as, turning to look at her husband, Charlotte asked coyly, "Do you remember a certain promise you made to me a few weeks ago?"

"Any promise I have made, my dear love, I shall most certainly fulfill . . ."

"Then you begin straightaway to grow mustachios . . . with them, you will look still more handsome . . ."

For reply, she found herself being taken in his arms, his lips fiercely claiming hers, with a whispered, "If that is what you wish, you little torment . . . my little *liebchen* . . . my very own little *liebchen*."

The overpowering heat of the June sun was so terrific that the good folk of Saxe Meiningen were grateful for this unexpected holiday in celebration of Princess Ida's wedding to the Duke of Weimar.

Throughout the whole five hundred square miles of the little state, they were congregating in every available open space, the market places, the parks and the village greens. They came to meet their friends and relatives; to dance and sing and to enjoy their share of the food and drink provided by their beloved ruler, the bride's widowed mother, Duchess Eleanor, now Regent until her son Bernard became of age. They added a gay touch to the festivities; the women in their bright-colored skirts and embroidered blouses along with their men-folk wearing equally gay shirts tucked into their knee-length breeches.

It was too hot to dance, and the bandsmen playing

wedding airs and folksongs were grateful for the barrels of beer placed at their disposal, as were the perspiring bell-ringers, glad of a respite between carillons. Only the children, picturesque miniatures of their parents, seemed to have boundless energy dancing round in circles and singing games.

At Meiningen Castle itself, the crowds were even more dense and packed, for years ago, the Duke had given his people the right to use the courtyard as a meeting-place ... either for pleasure or business.

From an upstairs window, two girls looked down, and though it was now well into the afternoon, they were both still wearing their cotton morning wraps. Someone in the crowd espied them. The cry went up, "The princesses!" and immediately there were resounding cheers. A group of fiddlers struck up a merry jig and there they were, the stolid loyal citizens, little flaxen-haired girls and boys, village maidens and their beaus, plump mamas and papas, all jigging and twirling, with skirts and braided hair swinging out in wide circles.

The royal ladies waved again and again until the elder remarked warningly, "Had we not better be getting into our gowns? 'Twill soon be six o'clock and we mustn't keep your bridegroom waiting."

"Dear Adelaide, there's plenty of time. Rest assured Mama will see to it that we are not late. There's not a better organizer throughout all Europe."

Neither girl had any real claim to beauty, but all girls are beautiful on their wedding day and Princess Ida was no exception. Her face, radiant with excitement, was surrounded by clusters of fair, golden curls; curls that had taken Mama's *friseuse* more than two hours to put into position. Adelaide, however, while possessing the same fine golden hair, wore hers flat, parted down the middle with ringlets hanging either side her face, so arranged as to partly hide her bad complexion. She was the plainer of the two; small and thin, with an air of general melancholy.

"Adelaide?" Ida's voice sounded hesitant. "Are you very concerned that I am being married before you?"

For a moment there was silence. Then, "Am I such a bad actress? Can you really read my inner thoughts? The Bible teaches us that we should not covet, and, dear sister, I would have you know that I have no covetous thoughts about you . . . yet try as I will, I do rail against Fate."

Ida took her sister's hands. "I know, Adelaide. You have had a hard time as Mama's right hand, but my marriage could open many doors for you. In two years' time our brother, Bernard, comes of age, and then both you and Mama can take your ease. You can visit me, and I shall arrange that there are eligible princes to meet you."

"Princes? Where will they come from? Who will take me without a dowry? Mama has had to sell most of her jewelry to raise yours . . . and it is but paltry."

Ida shrugged her shoulders. "Yet 'tis curious that when money is needed for state affairs, it is always forthcoming from one source or another. Remember how Napoleon taxed us . . . and because we were afraid of losing our neutrality . . . we paid him."

"I remember. I remember his troops marching through. How we had to billet and feed them. I remember them being chased back leaving us to bury their dead, and tend their wounded . . . and to billet and feed their conquerors. Little wonder we are so poor."

Ida was now staring out of the small window up at the densely wooded mountain sides towering around the castle.

"When I was a little girl and Mama told us stories of the mountain trolls, I believed every word. How I longed for one to visit us; one who could turn straw into gold. I would fall asleep, hoping and hoping that some morning I would awake and find myself between silken sheets."

Adelaide laughed softly. ". . . And now the Duke of Weimar has worked the magic spell for you. You will have satin sheets in your bridal chamber?"

"Indeed. 'Twas one of my first purchases. How I've hated our cotton sheets and hangings . . . especially since the time I overheard the conversation between two Englishmen, staying here as Mama's guests."

"You never told me . . ."

"No. I should have been punished for eavesdropping and for having wicked, vain thoughts. They didn't realize that I understood English. They were discussing the bedrooms they had occupied. The one said his scullery-maid at home had a better room. The other, that he would not put his dog into such a place; no carpet on the floor; calico hangings on the bed and at the windows . . . the only piece of furniture a cheap wash-stand . . . and the hurtful part was that it was all true . . . and it's still true. Look at this room . . . our room . . . the bedroom of two royal princesses."

Ignoring Ida's outburst, Adelaide asked thoughtfully:

"Do you think the two Englishmen came with marriage negotiations . . . for either of us?"

"Quite possibly, but you know Mama would never consider a marriage with any of the English princes. They are the most evil and lecherous throughout all Europe." As her sister made no comment, she went on: "Their father is a madman . . . locked away in a padded room. The Prince Regent is reviled by his own people for his treatment of Princess Caroline, his wife. He had mistress after mistress . . . and his brothers are not much better."

"They have their mistresses, admittedly, but have not most kings and rulers and royal dukes? They are not necessarily vile . . ."

"Why, Adelaide, you surprise me. After all Mama's teaching, you could be tolerant towards them? They are so bad, that it is said that when the mad king dies, the country will rise up against the Regent . . . that there will be a revolution, far worse than that in France . . . that more heads will roll . . . more bloodshed . . ."

"Oh, Ida. Stop. Such talk on your wedding day!"

"You frighten me, Adelaide, showing partisanship towards the English dukes . . ."

"Set your fears at rest. They will not come seeking my

hand. They like a saucy, laughing eye; a voluptuous figure
. . . a white, plump bosom . . ."

"Then give me your promise, Adelaide . . ."

"Dear sister, should any of the mad king's sons come
awooing, I'll remember your warning . . ."

The door opened and their mother, fully robed for the
ceremony, followed by her personal dresser, came in.

"Not yet dressed? Quick, Louise. Get the princesses
into their gowns . . . and of what is Ida warning you?"

A smile passed between the sisters, and getting no
answer, the Duchess resignedly shrugged her shoulders.
Thank goodness, she was getting one daughter off her
hands.

II

Wrapped snugly in a huge fur cape, and leaning on her
husband's arm, Charlotte walked slowly down the front
steps of *Claremont* to where the ponies harnessed to her
garden chair restlessly pawed the ground, champing and
chafing at the rawness of the November day.

As Leopold helped her in, putting her feet into the
muff and tucking the fur rug around her, she jested:

"I must look like a huge, grizzly bear . . . all fur and
gross body."

"Charlotte . . . *doucement* . . . *doucement* . . ."

She laughed again, as with Leopold holding her hand,
and walking alongside, the ponies moved off in a slow
trot. "Always *doucement,* my darling, Doucement." With
a movement of her head she indicated the three men
walking behind, Dr. Stockmar, Sir Richard Croft and Mr.
Neville. "Need they walk so near that they can hear every
word we say? What are they afraid of? That I shall have
the child here in the garden chair?"

Leopold's eyes were full of reproach at her levity;
levity that he was always correcting, but for once, ignoring
it, he answered:

"You are now fifteen days overdue, my little *liebchen.*
Anything could happen . . . any time . . ."

". . . and that can't happen too soon. Oh, I am so hungry, beloved. So very hungry. For days and days I have had nothing to eat save bread and butter . . . bread and butter to eat and milk to drink. Truly, I've almost forgotten the taste of real food."

"Not much longer now, my love. 'Tis Sir Richard's orders and they must be obeyed. He knows what is best."

"I am beginning to doubt it. Does he think it best to bleed me so much? No wonder my child is late. Poor mite, he is too weak to make his entrance."

"Charlotte!" There was real consternation in her husband's voice. "You must not talk like that. Naturally I can understand you being distraught over the delay . . ."

"No. Only hungry." She laughed good-naturedly. "I have already given Mrs. Griffiths orders, that once my baby is here, I want something more substantial than her gruel . . ."

"Mrs. Griffiths is an excellent midwife. She will know what to give you and you must be guided by her. I take it the wet nurse is ready at call?"

"Of a certainty. Being the game-keeper's wife she is always to be found at the lodge. We've been most fortunate in securing her, for her children are always the picture of health."

"Then we need not pester ourselves on that score. Shall we go and see how our little Gothic Temple is progressing?"

For a while they lingered appraising the new structure. By spring it would be finished . . . a garden retreat . . . so very fashionable these days.

Charlotte in her furs was warm and cozy, but Leopold soon began to stamp his feet, suggesting that they should return indoors.

As the footmen held back the double doors, Charlotte turned to look over the grounds and gardens, the trees bare and stark against the grey winter afternoon; the lawns still rimed by last night's frost; the rosebeds all asleep until the spring.

"Doucement, my darling," she said softly. "I do so love

Claremont . . . whatever the season. It has brought us such perfect happiness, has it not?"

He took her arm and putting it through his, drew her close; looking down into her eyes, ". . . and in the years to come, my love, it will bring more happiness. When we see our children romping on the lawns, hear their voices . . . share their laughter . . . yes, my *liebchen, Claremont* will be still more beautiful."

It had become more than she could bear to join the gentlemen in the dining-room; to see and smell the rich roasts; to hear the tinkling decanters being passed around, while she ate nothing but bread and butter. Accordingly, she now dined in her own apartments, before going down to the drawing-room to await her husband, who still carried out the ritual they had established when they first came to *Claremont*.

Leaving the gentlemen to their port, Charlotte and any ladies who might be guests, would retire to the drawing-room, where, until Leopold joined her, she entertained them, playing on her new Broadwood piano. Then the ladies would discreetly retire, leaving them alone.

From behind the closed doors, they could be heard singing and laughing merrily as they composed their own sonnets. Then the music would stop, and the door flung open by Leopold, inviting them all to re-enter; but the piano lid was closed, as though the music belonged to them alone.

They revelled in their domestic privacy. From the onset, Leopold had queried the necessity of having ladies-in-waiting living in the house, and Charlotte had willingly agreed that the ladies' services should only be called upon for state occasions or visits to her father or grandparents.

In the same way, they had devised a ruling, never to sleep on a misunderstanding. If either had been put out by the other's behavior, it was openly discussed and all was forgiven, before the candles were snuffed.

At first she had resented that Dr. Stockmar was given living quarters at *Claremont*. She was afraid that his friendship with her husband would monopolize too much of his time, but as the months passed by, not only did she herself conceive a great liking for him, but came to realize the advantages of Leopold having a man friend . . . someone to accompany him on his daily shooting . . . a friendly rival at the billiard table . . . a discursive opponent, without becoming too argumentative. She wished Stocky had been one of the doctors for her confinement, but he had declined the honor saying that the Royal Family and the people would prefer English doctors.

Tonight as Leopold entered the drawing-room, she was playing and singing softly to herself and for a few moments he stood listening, but Charlotte's voice soon broke in on his thoughts. "I know you are there, darling. Come and sit down beside me . . . that is . . . if there is room."

"Charlotte . . . when will you learn not to jest about such things?"

"Never, my beloved Doucement. Never. My childhood was so mixed up . . . people quarreling around me . . . angry with me for trivial misdeeds, that I often made myself laugh . . . instead of weeping . . ."

"But that's all over now . . . We live for each other . . . for each other's happiness."

"I know. You brought the first real happiness into my life." As he seated himself beside her on the music stool, she pushed her fingers through his thick, black hair; then smoothed it down. "It needs combing," was her mock-caustic comment.

"That is your fault. You've neglected your wifely duties these last few days . . ."

"I've neglected much these last few days. I feel so woefully tired. Too tired to play or sing tonight. Instead, if you'll forgive me, I would prefer to go up to my room . . ."

He gave her his arm, looking at her apprehensively. "Are you all right? Do you think the time . . . ?"

She shook her head. "Not yet, Doucement . . . not yet."

As they left the room, the doctors waiting outside,

bowed gravely. As they lifted their heads and their eyes met, the same question could be read in them. "How much longer? How much longer?"

It was about three o'clock in the morning when Charlotte decided that she should ring for Mrs. Griffiths. Thank God the time had come. Leo was all loving concern. Shouldn't she get back into bed, instead of walking about the room? No, walking about eased the pain, and there was no danger of catching cold, a roaring fire burning in the big grate. As she heard the clatter of hooves, she pulled the curtain aside to peer out into the darkness. There they were, the *Claremont* grooms, in their dark green liveries and riding capes, dashing off to fetch the Privy Councillors, who were to be in attendance at the birth.

As she let fall the curtain, she remarked with her customary chuckle, "My lords won't thank me for getting them from their beds at this time of a cold morning," and then as an afterthought, "Wouldn't it be vastly amusing if the baby arrived before they did?"

"Not amusing, my love. If they are not here as witnesses, someone might dispute its legality . . ."

"Suggesting that it had been smuggled in, in a warming pan? That's the usual romantic tale, isn't it? Very well, my little Prince Coburg, wait until the gentlemen arrive. How about a wager, Leo, as to which gentleman will be the first to get here?"

She went into the adjoining breakfast-room where the dignitaries would wait until Mrs. Griffiths or Leo presented the baby to them. She poked a finger through Coco's cage and tickled the parrot, but Coco, with his head tucked under his wing, refused to be awakened at such an unearthly hour.

"Well, mind you keep that way," she admonished. "No bawling or shrieking while the gentlemen are here." She turned to Mrs. Griffiths, who was busying herself about the room ". . . *and I promise, too, dear Mrs. Griffiths, that I will neither bawl nor shriek.*"

"Lord bless you, Ma'am. If you want to give way to your feelings . . . you just let go. 'Tis no disgrace."

Wandering back to the bedroom, she found Leopold fully dressed and seated by the fire. It was a large room, situated on the corner of the house, simply furnished, but the soft green carpet with its pattern of white lovers' knots, gave it an air of luxurious comfort.

Between two windows stood the double bed with curtains of flowered chintz and headboard of blue pleated silk. Large wardrobes extended along the walls and a simple dressing-table completed the furnishings. On the other side, opposite the breakfast-room, was Leopold's dressing-room, now given over to Sir Richard Croft, the accoucher, who was still sleeping, Mrs. Griffiths assuring them that there was no point in waking him at this early stage.

Now the first carriage was heard to arrive, only two hours after the grooms' departure. It was Lord Bathurst, to be followed quickly by Lord Sidmouth and then the Archbishop of Canterbury together with the Bishop of London. The gentlemen were quickly ushered up to Charlotte's breakfast-room, where refreshments were awaiting them. Now it was seven o'clock, and dashing up came a chariot and four, bringing Dr. Baillie, with the Chancellor of the Exchequer hard on his heels.

At Leopold's insistence, Charlotte tried to rest, but her old restlessness was beginning to assert itself, as, leaning on his arm, she walked backwards and forwards across the room, occasionally peering out into the darkness, tapping her feet impatiently.

Already, reporters were at the gates of *Claremont,* notebooks in pocket, and little pots of ink hanging from their button-holes. Down at the *Bear Inn,* where they had been staying for several days, mine host was doing a flourishing trade, soothing their impatience and their numbed fingers and toes, with welcome punch and hot toddy.

All through the murky November day, representatives of the various embassies called to present their credentials, waiting in a downstairs room, to be at hand, to hear the great news, while upstairs, the fruitless travail went on, Leopold becoming more and more distracted, never for a second leaving Charlotte. Sometimes they would rest together on the bed, Charlotte rumpling her beloved Doucement's thick hair, promising it would be her first task, after the baby had been born.

It was during one of these respites, that she suddenly remarked, "Leopold, I have a confession to make."

He tried to silence her with a gentle kiss. "Whatever you've done, beloved, it is of no concern . . ."

"But it is. Promise me you will not be angry."

"As if I could . . . at a time like this . . ."

"Nor after?"

"Nor after."

She took a deep breath. "I wrote to my mother . . . to tell her of our child . . ."

"But *liebchen* . . . why should I object?"

"Because I signed a written promise that I would never again communicate with her . . ."

"Ah . . . but that was a promise made to your father . . . not to me . . ."

"Then you do not object?"

"On the contrary, I am glad that you did. A child should never forget its mother . . ."

"Then, Leopold . . . if she were ever to return to England, could we . . . could we invite her to stay here at *Claremont?*"

"She would always be welcome, subject to one condition . . ."

". . . and that?"

"That she did nothing to disrupt our happiness. If she did . . ."

Charlotte was quick to answer. "If she did, dear Doucement, I should be the first to ask her to go elsewhere . . ."

At four o'clock, as darkness closed in again, Sir Richard Croft issued a bulletin that the *Princess's illness was progressing in every respect as favorably as he could possibly wish.*

As the evening wore on, and there were no immediate signs of birth, Sir Richard and Dr. Baillie began to feel apprehensive, dispatching a groom to London to summon Dr. Sims, another well-known accoucher, who wasting no time, arrived in the early morning hours.

After his examination another bulletin was issued.

The labor of Her Royal Highness, the Princess Charlotte is going on very slowly but we trust favorably.

Signed: M. Baillie
Richard Croft
John Sims

It was Dr. Sims, who, on the assumption that he had been called in to give another opinion, suggested that the birth should be hastened by the use of forceps.

Richard Croft's face became a reddish purple.

"Never, Sir. Never. For one mother saved, twenty are murdered."

There was such determination in his voice, that Dr. Sims realized the futility of argument, but then why had Sir Richard sent for him?

All day long, another day of agony; agony of Charlotte's body; agony of Leopold's mind, Charlotte too weak to care, having had no food or sleep for two days and Leopold in a state of exhaustion and no desire to eat.

The dark, depressing day ended. The waiting reporters saw the lights appear in the windows, as the candles were lit. How much longer, they groaned. What was going on?

Up in the torture-filled room, Leopold refused to leave Charlotte, until about nine o'clock, when, Sir Richard assuring him that the birth was now imminent, he joined the others in the breakfast-room.

The door opened. All eyes looked up expectantly at Sir Richard Croft as he stood there, searching for words.

"Speak up, man. Speak. We're all waiting." It was Leopold, impatient anxiety in his voice.

With eyes downcast, the words came, hesitant and low.

"Her Royal Highness has been delivered of a male child. Stillborn."

There was a cry of anguish from Leopold as he rushed into the bedroom, where Dr. Sims was still working on the lifeless baby prince. He had plunged the little body into a bath of hot water; rubbed the tiny limbs with salt and mustard, but all to no purpose. He would have picked up the child to show it to Leopold, but Leopold had eyes and thoughts for no one but Charlotte, now being attended by Mrs. Griffiths.

Dropping on to his knees by the bedside he took her hands, bursting into a torrent of tears.

"My little *liebchen*. My little *liebchen*. All this suffering . . . and nothing . . . nothing." He couldn't go on, and Charlotte still too exhausted to talk, merely looked vacantly first at him and then at Mrs. Griffiths and the maids all weeping copiously, as they left the bedside. Then she managed to whisper wearily, *"We must all submit to the will of God."*

"But why? Why? Why had this to happen?" Leopold's voice was almost at shouting pitch.

Charlotte's mouth trembled. "I'm sorry, Doucement. So very, very sorry . . ."

He kissed her hands. "It is a grief we must share . . . help each other to bear, though God knows how."

"Next time," she whispered.

"Next time? Another time like this? Why should I expect you to endure it? I had absolute faith in Croft and Baillie . . . even when Stockmar contradicted their methods."

"I'm not afraid, Leo. As soon as I am strong again . . ."

He kissed her hands and then rested his cheek on hers. "Don't think about it now, my *liebchen*. Forget it. Sleep and get well again."

"And you, dear Doucement . . . you need sleep. Thank

you, dear one, for staying by my side. You do not love me the less . . . because . . . because I have failed you?"

Tenderly he put his arms around her and gently cradled her to him. "I love you still more because of our misfortune . . . now sleep."

Some of her old impishness had returned. "Not before I've had something to eat. Mrs. Griffiths promised me . . . ah, here she comes." She smiled feebly at the midwife, who in reply said with enforced gaiety, "Now see what I have brought you, Your Highness. Chicken broth. Toast. Gruel."

"Thank you, dear Griffiths. *Why, you've changed your dress. How smart you are, but why did you not put on the silk gown, my favorite?*"

"I'm saving that, Your Highness, for when your royal father comes to visit you. Now let me lift you into a comfortable position."

Leopold and the nurse together lifted and propped her up with pillows, Leopold taking the spoon to feed her.

She stopped him by placing her hand over his. "Dear, dear Doucement, please go to bed. I truly believe you are more exhausted than I. Griffiths can feed me. Then I promise, I shall quickly be asleep."

". . . but I hate being apart from you, yet as you say, I am indeed weary. Give me one promise, dear heart, that you will not fret."

"I promise." He embraced her long and tenderly. "Then sleep well, dear little wife." He kissed her again. "Till the morning, my *liebchen*."

Mrs. Griffiths followed him to the door. "Would you not like to see the child, Sir?" Dumbly he went with her into the breakfast-room, now deserted, save for the little waxen body in the cradle; the cradle that had been prepared with such loving care.

It was a big baby, perfectly formed, and beautiful in feature. A choking sob rose in Leopold's throat as he left the room by the other door. His son. His and Charlotte's son.

*   *   *

Charlotte did indeed enjoy her supper, and after a dose of camphor julep administered by Dr. Croft as a stimulant, she settled down to sleep, with Mrs. Griffiths in a truckle bed, near at hand.

It was soon after midnight, that Charlotte's cry of pain awoke the midwife, who quickly had all the doctors at the bedside. Their diagnosis was that the Princess had suffered a hemorrhage. By now she was tossing about in agony, yet at the same time, trembling with cold. Hot flannels and hot water bottles were instantly applied much to Dr. Stockmar's consternation. Calling Sir Richard aside he asked, "Surely, Sir, for a post-natal hemorrhage, should *not cold water be applied, not hot?*"

Sir Richard turned on him angrily. *"Are you . . . or I in authority here?"* Then he added tersely, *"I think you had better go fetch your master."*

"The pain. The pain," came Charlotte's reiterated moan. *"All here, all here,"* she gasped, pressing her stomach.

"Brandy. Hot wine," hissed Croft. Charlotte drank greedily. Anything that would deaden the pain. She looked Sir Richard full in the face. *"Am I in any danger, Sir?"* she asked tremulously.

Croft's answer came too quickly . . . too brusquely. *"No. No, Princess, but you must try to keep still."*

Charlotte's only answer was to draw up her legs in agony. Stockmar looked on in helpless pity. They had become close friends . . . almost as close as he was with Leopold. Without a word, he went to Leopold's room, and not bothering to knock, shook his sleeping master. "Sir! Wake up! The Princess is not so well."

Leopold muttered something unintelligible and rolled over. Again Stockmar tried to rouse him and again failed, not knowing that Dr. Croft had given him an opiate. It was no use. Perhaps he could be of more service to Charlotte.

As he entered the bedroom again, Dr. Baillie said facetiously, *"Ah, Princess, here comes an old friend of yours."*

Stockmar moved quickly to the bedside where Charlotte seized his hand. *"They have made me tipsy, Stocky."*

For a few seconds he held her hand, long enough to feel the racing pulse, long enough to know that Leopold must get here quickly, before . . .

He dashed back to Leopold's room, but try as he would, he could not rouse him. Back to Charlotte, to say the comforting word if need be . . . she seemed to be rallying a little . . . he must get Leo here . . . but even as he moved to leave the room again, he was stopped by her anguished cry, *"Stocky. Stocky."*

With the other doctors he stood and watched helplessly . . . watched her last convulsive movements . . . heard her last breath leave the torn, bruised body.

With the application of cold water, alternated by sharp slaps on the Prince's face, Stockmar had finally succeeded in rousing Leopold, but so far his words could not penetrate the bemused mind.

With his arms around his master, Stockmar almost dragged him to Charlotte's room but outside the door, Leopold would have collapsed had there not been a chair in the vicinity. Now he was sufficiently awake to realize something was amiss. "Go . . . Stockmar . . . tell the Princess . . . I will be with her in a few moments."

Allowing him a short respite, Stockmar then returned and, seeing that Leopold was now more alert, took his arm and gently led him to Charlotte's bedside.

It was then that the full impact of all Stockmar's efforts to rouse him, broke with sword-edge clarity. Charlotte was lying back on her pillows, wearing a look of serene peace . . . the peace of death. Charlotte was dead. It couldn't be true. She couldn't be dead. He fell on his knees, seizing the hands that Mrs. Griffiths had already placed together, passionately kissing them, then her arms, calling out frantically, "Charlotte, come back. You cannot leave me. Charlotte, my very own little *liebchen*, come back," and when there was no answer, and no one spoke, he burst into uncontrolled sobbing and weeping.

No one attempted to interrupt him. No one tried to

comfort him. They knew he was beyond comfort. Mrs. Griffiths and her maids crept silently out of the room, their own grief increased by that of their master. The doctors stood embarrassed and apprehensive. Then they, too, left the room. Outside the door, Stockmar waited in the chair just vacated by the Prince, while all the household, unable to sleep, tried to shut out the most terrible sound in the world . . . the weeping and sobbing of a man, bereft forever of the woman he loved.

How long Leopold stayed in the room, Stockmar never knew, for he eventually fell into a doze, but at the opening of the door, was quickly on his feet to see his master stumbling from the room, staring around him as though dazed.

In the brief time he had spent in that room beside his dead wife, a pitiful change had come over him. His ashen face, ravaged with grief, seemed to have taken on a hollowness, pronounced by the red-rimmed eyes.

He stared vacantly at Stockmar, like a child, unsure of himself, then finally spoke . . . in a voice quavering between incredulity and hopelessness. *"I am now quite desolate. Promise me to always stay with me."*

Stockmar took his arm. *"I promise, Sir. Come now to bed."*

Leopold allowed himself to be led away, to have his bedrobe removed, to be put into bed, but as Stockmar was about to leave, he called him back.

"Do you recall your promise?"

"I do, Sir. I will never leave you as long as you need me . . . love me . . . and I can be of use to you."

All England wept and after the tears came despondency. Gone were all the hopes of a young queen with wider and more visionary ideas; only a string of middle-aged, lecherous, extravagant roués remained. Was it too much to hope that one of them might marry, and so beget an heir?

1

There was much curiosity and a certain jubilation as the Duke of Kent's footmen brought back to the kitchen all the breakfast dishes . . . all untouched . . . and most astounding of all, a full pot of tea, freshly brewed. What had happened?

The first footman, however, was too busy looking after his tea to volunteer any immediate information. After having shared the tea with the head servants, the leaves had to be removed from the pot and put out to dry, for he had a waiting market for them, despite the fact that they made but a weak infusion. Then, and not till then, did he begin to tell his story, laconically remarking, "No sooner had Madame seated herself, picked up the news-sheet, than she goes off into this swoon."

There was a chorus of unbelief. "Madame swooned? Is she ill? Whatever did His Grace do?"

"Oh, he was all concern. Patting her hand and whispering, while I rang for her woman. As soon as she could stand, back upstairs she went, weeping and moaning."

"But whatever could have brought on her distress?"

"Ah." The lackey tapped his nose knowingly. "I knew something would happen as soon as I read that news-sheet . . ."

"Since when have you found time to read the news-sheet?"

"Long before they come down. I read it every morning."

"While you have us scuttling round doing all the work . . ."

"A man should know what's going on in the country . . ."

"Well? What is going on? What could there be in the news-sheet to upset Madame? Stop being so devilishly tormenting."

"Well, we all know, the relationship between the Duke and Madame . . ."

There was a chorus of groans from his listeners. "Tell us something we don't know. We are all well aware, she's been his mistress for more than twenty years . . ."

"That's just it. This news-sheet puts out in big lettering that the time has come for all the royal dukes to form proper, legal relationships . . . in other words that they should marry . . . and produce heirs for the throne . . ."

"Marry! The Duke of Kent to marry!"

An awkward silence filled the big kitchen. "Poor lady. She has always been a kind mistress . . ."

Somebody sniggered . . . "And that's just her position, and she knows only too well, that she and the Duke must part . . ."

"Do you think the Duke can bring himself to send her away . . . after all these years?"

With Madame leaving the breakfast-room, Edward picked up the fallen news-sheet. The headlines met his gaze. He scanned the opening paragraph.

So that was the cause of Julie's swoon. Poor, dear Julie. How long had they been together? Twenty-seven years? They had been happy years, for Julie never questioned his wishes . . . she was so dutiful, implicitly obedient. Now she knew without being told, that they must part . . . the country was demanding it. Yet he knew he would never find a wife so complacent, so amiable as dear, gentle Julie.

The prospect of a change elated him. He felt he couldn't sit down and breakfast alone, and pulling the bell, ordered that the table should be cleared.

He went over to peer at himself in the overmantel. A little too stout, maybe, but he could reduce his eating and drinking and although he had formerly scorned to wear a wig, it might be advantageous to cover up his bald head.

It would indeed be exciting to have a young bride . . . to have children . . . to recapture his youth. Already he could feel the years slipping away. Then he gave a deep sigh. It was going to be so cruel dismissing Madame Julie St. Laurent; to send her back to her family in Canada, especially now, that she was no longer young, but he would see to it that she had a good settlement. How much would she need to live in decent comfort? He would see his dear friend, Maria Fitzherbert. She would be able to advise him on such a delicate matter.

Maria Fitzherbert had already had one royal visitor that morning, but she listened attentively as the Duke presented his problem, seeking advice and sympathy. Although now turned sixty, Marie was as alert in mind and spirit as she had ever been; and by judicious living, was still the acknowledged Queen of Assemblies both in Brighton and London. It was now seven years since she and the Regent had parted; years during which they haughtily cut each other dead, whenever they happened to meet, yet deep down, she still hoped that when he did become King, he would repeal the Royal Marriage Act and announce their secret marriage. Did she still love him? Nowadays, she didn't probe the wound. What was the use, when he took mistress after mistress?

"So you do see, dear Mrs. Fitzherbert, that it is imperative that I should marry."

Roused from her reverie, Maria's monosyllable reply sounded sharp and tart.

"Why?"

"Why? Why, because . . . because it is my duty . . . to have an heir . . ."

"But the Duke of Clarence is before you . . . and as you know, Sir, he is quite capable of begetting heirs . . ."

"But he has no desire to marry. Did he not say so after the death of Mrs. Jordan?"

"Pooh! Sentimental poppycock, rising from a guilty

conscience, made worse by his son Henry dying out in India. Yes, your brother William should take a wife."

"But who will marry him? How many refusals has he not already suffered?"

"That may be so, but circumstances have now changed. I'll guarantee there's quite a few foreign princesses fretting and fuming for the chance of being queen of England . . . or mother of a future ruler."

"But how many will relish the thought of being step-mother to a house full of bastards?"

"La, Sir! They're all growing up now. The boys will take their place in the world and the girls will marry."

"Nevertheless, I intend to be first in the field . . ."

Maria laughed gently. "Then you must waste no time, Sir, for William is already looking around the German marriage market . . ."

"The devil he is! When did you hear this?"

"Only an hour ago . . . and from the Duke himself. Like you, he protests his regret at having to give up his bachelor estate . . ."

"But I do, Madam. Indeed I do. It tears the very heart out of me, having to part from Madame St. Laurent. It is only the call of duty that bids me . . ."

"Fiddlesticks, Sir! The call of duty couldn't have come at a more opportune moment. Madame growing old . . . your comfortable companionship becoming a bore. I told William the same. Like you, he needs a woman in his life and this time he must marry . . . but only from a sense of duty! Duty! Bah! Duty!"

As she watched his carriage drive away, she mused, "Duty. I married for love . . . but what did it bring me? Could it be, that marrying for duty might bring that elusive thing, happiness?"

Adolphus, Duke of Cambridge, Vice-Regent of Hanover, was lost in deep thought. Before him lay the letter giving the grim details of his niece Charlotte's death and funeral. Poor, dear little fair-haired Charlotte. He could only envisage her as the gay tomboy he had known when

he had left England in 1813, a tomboy just beginning to
show the signs of a lovely young woman, ready and eager
to fall in love. He had always felt a certain responsibility
for her, in that she was the child of that ill-fated marriage
. . . for it was he who had suggested Cousin Caroline of
Brunswick as consort for the Prince of Wales.

What a sorry mess the English succession now faced!
Three of his brothers were married, but all childless . . .
as to the others, up to now, all perfectly satisfied with less
regular unions . . . how would they react to this disas-
ter?

Take William, for instance. Some months back, this
unpredictable brother of his had written asking him to
look around the German princesses, and select him a
suitable wife. When he had written extolling the virtues of
nineteen-year-old Princess Augusta, youngest daughter of
the landgrave of Hesse-Cassell, what did William do, but
write back jesting that from the tone of the letter, he,
Adolphus, was in love with Augusta. Why didn't he marry
her?

Why not indeed? The idea of marriage had gone sour
on him since that disastrous betrothal to Frederica, his
cousin, and widow of a Prussian prince. The engagement
had been publicly announced with the blessing of his
father, George III, when for no given reason, she jilted
him and married the Prince of Solms. Unfortunately,
within a very short time, Frederica again found herself a
widow, and despite the manner in which she had insulted
the English monarchy, who should step forward and rush
her once again to the altar, than his brother Ernest, Duke
of Cumberland. Not that Adolphus had any real regrets,
for the lady had not hesitated to cuckold both her former
husbands to such extent, that his mother refused to receive her at the English court.

Now the idea of marriage was again stirring within
him. Why should he not marry Princess Augusta? He was
the youngest of the royal dukes, not yet forty-five . . . the
only one not crippled with debt . . . fond of the arts and
quiet living . . . popular with the Hanoverians . . . yes, he

had much to offer a young wife. Why should he not provide England with an heir?

The carriage was traveling at a rapid pace, rattling over the narrow, mountainous road leading to Coburg. The occupants, two gentlemen muffled in traveling capes and rugs, spoke hardly a word, but Stockmar was now feeling happier than he had done since the death of Charlotte. He had at last managed to rekindle a spark of interest in his master's blacked-out world.

Attempting to make conversation, he had happened to mention the rumors going around that the royal dukes were all seeking wives. Who would be the first to reach the altar? The cartoonists were already finding the Royal Marriage Stakes a good subject for their vituperations.

There had been no immediate reply . . . then there had dawned that familiar look in Leopold's eyes . . . the look that meant he was planning and scheming. That was just a week ago, and now, traveling incognito, they were making a secret visit to Leopold's home.

As they traveled through the cold January afternoon, the darkness quickly closing in, Stockmar hoped and prayed Leopold's scheme would be fruitful.

It was not that he regretted his promise to Leopold, but life at *Claremont* had been almost unbearable. Christmas, always such a gay festivity here in Germany, had been a mockery. There had been no entertaining and the Prince had refused all invitations. Only the Regent's sisters had called, weeping when they came and weeping as they departed.

As their carriage passed through the big iron gates of the Schloss Ehrensburg Palace, sighs of audible relief were heard from both men.

"You sound, Stockmar, as though you are truly glad to be back on your native soil."

"Of a certainty, Sir . . . and you too, I presume."

"My heart is now in England. Never forget that, Stockmar. This is but a duty visit . . . You still agree with me, I take it, that this would be a good match?"

"An excellent match, Sir, for all concerned."

The crunch and grind of their coach coming to a halt in front of the palace was the only herald of their arrival, but a couple of flunkeys on duty in the main hall were quickly down the long flight of stone steps, while another hastened to inform the Dowager Duchess Augusta that unexpected callers had arrived.

Leopold, bowed and dejected, followed by Stockmar, entered his childhood home, but it wasn't until more candles had been brought, that the footman recognized the Prince, and leading the way to the family drawing-room, made the announcement.

Startled, the Duchess and her daughter, the widowed Victoire, rose to their feet, Leopold almost falling into his mother's arms.

"My son," she murmured, with tears coursing down her cheeks, " 'tis good to see you. Welcome home." Oh, God, she thought, how ill and haggard he looks. What could have brought him here?

Now he was kissing Victoire, whispering that he wished to see her alone as soon as possible. In the background, a boy of about thirteen and a little girl some years younger were being restrained by their governess from joining their elders, but it was Leopold who spoke out, "Since when were you not allowed to kiss your Uncle Leopold?"

A look of pain crossed his face as the little girl rushed forward and threw herself into his arms.

"Oh, Uncle Leopold. I have so missed you . . . and I said the prayer, often and often."

Her mother sharply interrupted. "Feodora, your brother Charles also wishes to greet his uncle . . ."

Pushed aside, the child began in a whispering voice to recite the prayer she had been taught when Uncle Leopold had married Aunt Charlotte.

"O thou Ruler of the Universe, grant him a happy family life, which in high places is very rare, and may Charlotte, when she ascends the throne, remain the same loving wife."

But God hadn't listened and Aunt Charlotte and her little baby had died and Grandmother and Mother and all the other ladies, and she too, had worn black dresses for days and days and days . . . Perhaps Uncle Leopold had come to cheer them up.

"So I've come, Victoire, to point out to you all the advantages of marrying into the English Royal Family. Without making it too obvious, that as your brother, I was the chief sponsor of the match, I have let fall, in the right places of course . . . your excellent qualities as a . . ."

"Spare my blushes, dear brother. While it might be an excellent match, what about this woman with whom he has had such a long acquaintance? I have no desire to play second fiddle to a worn-out mistress."

"There is no fear of that. She has already wisely taken her *congé* and has retired into a French convent."

Victoire laughed cruelly. "A place of correction for her no doubt . . . to pay penance for her long sinning . . ."

"Listen, Victoire, for I must return tomorrow. I come but to stress . . . to insist that you accept this offer of marriage. You'll never get a better. The English government is generous . . . the Duke's allowance is to be increased on marriage, and with the Duke of Kent as my brother-in-law, my position in England will be strengthened. You do see the advantages, dear sister?"

"In many respects, yes . . . but there are disadvantages. You yourself dislike the Regent . . . and his brothers . . ."

". . . Save the Duke of Kent." For a moment there was silence. Then, "Would it influence you at all if I were to tell you that . . . that . . . my beloved Charlotte, on more than one occasion, vowed how she would like to see you married to her Uncle Kent. He was, she insisted, very kind to her mother."

It was the first time Charlotte had been mentioned, but Victoire dare not pursue several questions that rose in her mind. Was it true that the autopsy had revealed several diseased organs? Was it true that Sir Richard Croft had committed suicide, so overcome with remorse and the general odium being poured upon him?

She put her arm through his, drawing him to her. "Very well, Leopold. Provided my trustees agree, and that the terms of the marriage contract satisfy me . . . I'll take your advice. Now tell me, why must you hurry back?"

"Because I prefer that neither the Regent nor the government know of my visit to you. Stockmar and I have traveled incognito and we'll return that way. The other dukes are also looking for wives and I would that you made the best match of all."

"Match-maker," she teased.

His lips tightened and his eyes hardened. "That is all there is left for me."

Princess Adelaide's thoughts were far from the book of devotions now lying in her lap. Two hours ago, an outrider had brought the news that her sister, Ida, the Duchess of Weimar, was on her way to visit Meiningen. Adelaide could guess the purpose of her visit, and usually so gentle and calm in acceptance of events, good or evil, she resented the uninvited guest. The afternoon wore on, dull and purposeless, save for ordering a room to be prepared for the Duchess. Oh, to escape . . . to have a home of her own . . . a life of her own . . . a husband . . . children.

Lost in a daydream, she did not hear the carriage pull up in the courtyard, and it was not until the shabbily dressed footman flung open the door and announced the Duchess, that Adelaide was aware of her arrival.

Immediately they were in each other's arms, Adelaide forgetting all her rancor.

"What brings you here, Ida, through all this heavy April rain?"

"As if you didn't know." Ida was now removing her cape and hood, revealing the richly embroidered gown . . . a gown such as she never possessed when a mere princess of Meiningen.

"Well, perhaps what I meant to ask was why you have come with such haste . . . leaving behind your baby." She moved to pull the bell . . . "Mama asked that she should be told immediately you arrived . . ."

"No. Leave her for a while. It is to you I want to talk . . ."

Adelaide, anxious to put off the awkward questions, again hedged. "Let me ring for a dish of tea . . ."

"No. That too can wait. Oh, Adelaide, how could you be so foolish . . . ?"

"Foolish?"

"Don't pester me, Adelaide. You know well what I mean. Negotiations, I understand, have been received from the Duke of Clarence . . . negotiations asking for your hand in marriage . . . and what's more, I have it on good authority that both you and Mama are giving them favorable consideration?"

As Adelaide made no reply, Ida went on with a sorrowful tone in her voice. "And after promising me that you would have nothing to do with the odious creatures from England . . . a promise made to me on my wedding day. Do you not remember?"

"I remember . . . but I did not promise not to negotiate . . . I promised to remember your warning."

". . . and now you're disregarding it. Adelaide, can't you see the folly of it? The man's a monster. He has ten children . . ."

"That doesn't make him a monster, Ida. I hear that he has a great love for them . . . that he is an excellent father."

". . . but all he wants from you is a legal child . . ."

"Which as his wife, I would have been proud to give him. Oh, Ida, Ida . . ." And to her sister's distress, Adelaide burst into tears.

"What is it, Adelaide? What has happened? If, after searching your heart you found you could not marry him, believe me, sister, you have done the wisest thing."

There was a touch of hysteria in Adelaide's voice as she attempted to answer, a mixture of sobs and shaky laughter. "It's . . . it's so funny to listen to you . . . and then to tell you . . . he has broken off negotiations . . ." Her voice trailed away in a silly giggle.

For a moment Ida was silent, then she burst out indignantly, "How dare he! How dare he treat you, Princess Adelaide of Meiningen, with such . . . such base behavior?"

Adelaide had still not recovered her composure. "Because . . . because the English government will not increase his allowance by more than £6,000 a year. He demanded £19,000 . . ."

". . . and most probably needs it with that brood to maintain . . ."

Adelaide was now drying her eyes. "He has refused the £6,000 . . . so that is why . . ."

"It is still a gross insult. Nevertheless, you are well rid of him. I am glad. Now ring for Mama and that dish of tea."

On the third day of her visit, having now satisfied herself that Adelaide was out of imminent danger, the Duchess Ida decided to return to Weimar.

There was much kissing and hugging with loving messages sent to the Duke and dear little baby Louise, before the carriage moved out of the castle courtyard.

As they slowly walked indoors, the Duchess Eleanor put her arm around Adelaide. "Come into the library, child. The courier brought a letter from England this morning . . ."

"From the Duke of Clarence, Mama?"

"Yes, he is desirous of reopening negotiations . . ."

"Why? Has he been granted more money?"

"No . . . it is just that he wishes to marry . . . you."

In the library, with its shelves of books lining the walls, most of them collected by her father, who had taught her to love learning, she seated herself beside her mother, and asked, frankly:

"And what do you think, Mama?"

The Duchess shrugged her shoulders. "You are of an age, Adelaide, when you should decide for yourself. I will not take any part in persuading you either way."

Adelaide had no hesitation. "Then I say, 'Yes,' Mama. I wish to marry the Duke."

There was a pregnant silence in the room. At last the Duchess spoke. "Yes. Considering all things, I think 'tis better to marry than remain here. Your brother, Bernard, will marry . . . and will want this castle. We know the

Duke of Clarence lacks morals and manners . . . but he has reached middle age . . . he is desirous of an heir . . . and let us hope, settled domesticity. You could give him all these things."

"I will try, Mama. I will try." Then, as an afterthought, "You did not tell Ida of this fresh negotiation?"

"No, Adelaide, no. She would only have fussed and tried to talk you out of it. Once you are married she will accept the fact . . . and the Duke."

2

It was devilishly galling that his brother Adolphus had beaten him to the altar, and that he and his pretty little girl bride had already left Hanover, *en route* for England. Not that he had any real cause for anxiety . . . Adolphus was well down in the line of accession.

Such were the thoughts still rankling in the Duke of Kent's mind as he stood by the side of his bride, Victoire, Duchess of Meiningen; she in her virginal shimmering bridal gown, he perspiring and uncomfortable in his heavy tight-fitting uniform of a field marshal.

When the castle guns of Coburg announced that they were man and wife, his first thoughts were to get out of the Riesensaal, away from the glare and heat of the two hundred and eighty-eight candles flickering above him. Thank God, he and his duchess would also soon be on their way to England, although the fact that his mother was insisting on another wedding ceremony as soon as they arrived was another source of irritation. One thing, however, afforded him great satisfaction. He had outdistanced William, who was still negotiating for the hand of Adelaide of Saxe-Mciningen.

The crowd outside Rundle and Bridges, the city jewelers, had been quick to gather when they saw the royal carriage waiting with full complement of liveried, powdered flunkeys. Who was within? What were they buying? More jewels to put round thcir women's necks? Did they never give a thought to the empty bellies of their subjects? Laughter, sneers, shouts and catcalls swelled to a frightening crescendo as the shop door opened and the proprietor, with deep profound bows bade farewell to his customers; customers who had spent with generous largesse.

A young lady of about eighteen, clung timorously to her escort, a handsome man in his mid-forties, while the flunkeys closed round them protectingly, canes in hand, as others formed a cordon to keep the pathway clear.

Then as someone recognized the newly-wed Duke and Duchess of Cambridge, the cry went up, and the boos changed to cheers. Adolphus, the youngest of the royal brothers, was a "decent fellow" and as for his bride, although she was another German, well . . . she was but a chit.

As the coach moved slowly away lest the horses should trample on the pressing mob, Augusta spoke tremulously to her husband, "I was so afraid. I thought they were going to attack us . . ."

"*Nein . . . nein . . . mein liebchen.* Everyone loves a bride . . . you have nothing to fear."

By mid afternoon the Duchess had so far recovered her composure, as to decide on a saunter in Kew Gardens, and accompanied by her ladies-in-waiting, strolled slowly along the tree-lined walks, her ridiculously minute parasol held up to shade her face from the hot June sun.

She had walked but little distance, before she became aware that another lady, obviously of high rank, in that she too had a retinue of ladies, was approaching her with curious scrutiny. As they were about to pass, with only the slightest of bows, the stranger exclaimed in German,

"Pray, Ma'am, do forgive me, but are you not Princess Augusta of Hesse-Cassel?"

Augusta hesitated. The lady was middle-aged, heavily painted and wore her dress far too décolleté for mid-afternoon. She carried herself with a certain rakish jaunt of her shoulders; a semi-impertinent smile playing about her sensuous mouth.

It was distinctly against protocol to speak to anyone who had not been presented to her, but there was something familiar about this lady . . . she felt sure she had met her before . . . and she spoke German.

Seeing her hesitation, the lady went on, with a chuckling laugh, "May I present myself? I am the Duchess of Cumberland. You and I are sisters-in-law, for you are the Duchess of Cambridge, are you not?"

Augusta hesitated no longer. Here was someone she could really talk to . . . in German . . . for as yet, not being able to carry on a conversation in English, she found social occasions very dull and boring.

She looked around, beaming. "See! There is an arbor over there. Do let us sit down and talk. Were you at our wedding ceremony yesterday? I do not recall seeing you, Ma'am."

"*Nein. Nein,* little sister. Call me Frederica. I might be twice your age, but we are now very closely related. No, I was not at your wedding, for the very simple reason that I was not invited . . . nor was my husband, Ernest."

Augusta frowned. "But why not? The Regent was there . . . the Duke of Clarence . . . the princesses . . . and of course, the Queen."

"Did she not confide the reason of our absence?"

"No. Indeed, no."

"How odd. The old cow dotes on gossip as much as any of us. The truth is, she does not approve of me . . . nor of Ernest, and will have neither of us at her prissy, prudish court."

Puzzled, Augusta persisted, "But why?"

Frederica shrugged her shoulders. "Perhaps because Ernest is my third husband . . . perhaps because gossip says that I poisoned the first two . . . perhaps because I have always attracted lovers . . . including your dear Adolphus."

The color left Augusta's face. "I do not understand. Surely you do not imply . . ."

"Now I'm spoiling love's young dream, am I not? Do not fret yourself, child. You were still in the nursery when Adolphus and I were betrothed . . ."

"Betrothed? I never knew . . ."

"He was to have been my second husband. Everyone was in such full approval. Then I met the Prince of Solms, and . . . well . . . there was no gainsaying him. He was so persistent that he persuaded me to break off the match. *Gott in Himmel!* What a fuss there was!"

She paused as though reminiscing within herself. "Then he died . . . within a few years of our marriage . . . and though I would have returned to the arms of my dear, heartbroken Adolphus . . . he would have none of me."

"Perhaps he was no longer heartbroken," interrupted Augusta, with a sudden show of spirit.

"Perhaps not. That is why I was quick to accept Ernest when he asked for my hand. One way or another, I was determined to be an English duchess, but his mother, that old, dried-up monkey of a woman, was furious and forbade us to come to England."

"But you are here? You have defied her?"

"Why not? The Regent and Ernest are good friends, why should we be denied? Are the other royal dukes, their wives, their mistresses, the princesses . . . are any of them of such purity that they can afford to cast stones?"

There was such venom and scorn in her voice that Augusta was at a loss to reply and was compelled to listen as the bitter, sarcastic voice went on. "You've much to learn . . . and I could teach you. Two at least of the unmarried princesses have had children . . ."

"Oh no, Ma'am. I must not listen . . ."

"No? It doesn't make pretty hearing, does it, but it's true. What about the Duke of Clarence shortly to marry, and his family of ten bastards? What about the Duke of Kent? A lifetime spent with a mistress, and then with the hope of a throne, or a throne for his heir, she is cast aside? All of them . . . and every one of them, is as guilty as my husband . . . and as for the Regent . . . ! How much do you know about Mrs. Fitzherbert and his wife Caroline?"

Frederica's guttural voice had taken on a loud shrill note, causing passers-by to look towards the arbor with curious stares. In an attempt to lower the Duchess's voice, Augusta almost whispered, "Nothing, Ma'am . . . well, very little, save for cousin Caroline's scandalous behavior."

"Which she, poor fool, has been driven to. Tormented and denied her own child . . . and now, because that child is dead, this crazy rush among the brothers to marry . . . to see who can produce the first candidate for the throne."

Augusta spoke with childish hauteur. "We are not concerned with any rush. The Duke of Cambridge is the youngest brother . . ."

"But the healthiest! Who knows what Dame Fortune has up her sleeve? I don't mind admitting we have our hopes. Ernest is next in succession after the Duke of Kent. I already have six brats by my previous marriages, but I rather fancy a little English princeling . . . if only to make Her Majesty squirm . . ."

White and shaken Augusta rose. "I must go." She motioned to her ladies, continuing, "We are only staying in London until after the weddings of the Dukes of Kent and Clarence. Then we return to Hanover. So I will bid you farewell."

Frederica laughed. "What a pretty way of saying you do not wish to see me again . . . but you will . . . either here or in Hanover. In the meantime, remember me to our mother-in-law. She'll have a heart attack when she learns that we have met."

The Duchess of Cumberland's prediction came true. The Queen did have a heart attack, so severe, that for several days her life was in danger, during which time the

Regent insisted that Ernest take himself and his gossiping wife back to the Continent as quickly as possible.

The two carriages spanking down Albemarle Street, followed by several baggage wagons, caused the few citizens about to stop and stare, especially when they saw that all the vehicles bore the royal crest. Finally, when the entourage pulled up outside Grillons Hotel, a crowd quickly gathered.

From the first carriage came two ladies; one young and one old, while from the second, two ladies and two gentlemen stepped down, obviously in waiting on the occupants of the first.

The gentlemen were quickly up the hotel steps speaking with the manager, who by his obsequious manner, was obviously much flattered that his hotel should be patronized by such important visitors.

The best suite of rooms was awaiting them, but as soon as they were alone in the big, well-furnished salon, the Duchess Eleanor could no longer keep silent.

"Mein Gott! But this is an insult! Not only did the Duke of Clarence refuse to come to Meiningen, but it was also too much trouble to meet us when we arrived in his country . . . and now . . . London . . . and still no one to meet us . . . and boarded out in a public hotel, when I did at least expect that we should stay either at *Carlton House* or St. James's Palace," and the poor distraught lady burst into tears.

Adelaide put a comforting arm around her mother. "It will be all right, Mama. We are in a foreign country now. Their ways are different . . ."

"That is what pesters me . . . that this is to be your country . . . that there is no welcome for you . . ."

"Let us eat, Mama. We are all hungry and tired. Sooner or later, someone must call on us."

". . . they think that because they have paid our traveling expenses, they can treat us like paupers . . ."

"Nonsense, Mama. You are overwrought. Let your ladies take you to your room . . ."

". . . and miss whoever might call? No. I stay here. A dish of tea will suffice me."

They had not long to wait. Freiherr Von Konitz, legal adviser to the Duchess, came in to whisper that a certain Major George Fitzclarence was below, having been sent by his father, the Duke of Clarence to pay his respects to the ladies.

The Duchess paled. The Princess felt her usually wan face take on a heightened color. For a second, no one spoke. Then the Duchess ejaculated, "Another insult! How dare he send . . . the son of that . . . that woman. . ."

"Mother! We should see the gentleman. No good would be gained from sending him away." She motioned to the Freiherr, who silently left the room.

"Adelaide! I will not stay to meet him!" The Duchess was almost beside herself with indignation.

"Mother. Please. Always you have insisted on the perfection of my manners. At least let me show this gentleman the success of your teaching."

Adelaide watched the door with bated breath. Then he was announced. "Major George Fitzclarence," and the Freiherr was making the presentation.

The first thought that struck her was that he must be about her age . . . and then that he was devastatingly handsome both in feature and figure. Here was her future husband's eldest son. Could it be possible that her bridegroom, though thirty years her senior, might be handsome in his maturity?

As George Fitzclarence bowed low, his father's words were echoing round his brain. "I'm scared to meet her. Poor young thing . . . to be tied to a creature like me. Go and visit her . . . break the ice . . . she might feel easier when she has seen you."

If his father was scared, how about this plain, wan little woman, but as he looked up and met her smile, gentle and welcoming, it was he who became flustered, seeing her easy control of the situation.

"My father, Ma'am, will be along later this evening, but until he can get here . . . he . . . he begged me to apologize for his tardiness . . ." His shyness threatened to get the better of him.

"Pray be seated, Sir. This is indeed a pleasant surprise." He groped for the right opening conversation.

"Did—did you have a pleasant journey, Ma'am?"

"Most delightful, Sir. Your English countryside is truly entrancing . . ."

"Ah, then, you will love *Bushey!*"

"*Bushey?* Vhat is *Bushey?*"

"The Duke's country house. We all love it . . . We spent our childhood there . . ." He stopped suddenly, checking his enthusiasm.

She regarded him, smiling. "Tell me more about *Bushey.*"

"Oh, you must see it to appreciate it. It has everything, and not too far from London, when the Regent is at *Carlton House.* Almost every night then, there is an assembly at some house or other . . . if not an assembly, an opportunity to go to the theater. Do you like the theater, Ma'am?"

Again, the sharp indrawn breath, as he realized he had made another mistake, but Adelaide pretended not to notice.

"You mean the play? In my country, singers and dancers are more popular, but I look forward to visiting your theater . . ."

His smile spoke his gratitude. What a kind, understanding creature she was. Now what could they talk about? He was always tongue-tied when in a lady's company. Minnie Seymour was constantly teasing him about it. Thinking of her, he was astounded when the Princess broke in on his thoughts. "Are you married, Major Fitzclarence?"

Taken off his guard, he could only stammer, "No, Ma'am. Oh no. No." Then to cover up his abrupt reply he added, attempting a jocular tone, "The lady to whom I have given my heart does not return my affection."

Before she could reply, Herr Von Effa came into the room, and first turning to the Duchess and then the Princess, said breathlessly, "His Royal Highness, the Regent, is below."

All rose to their feet and George Fitzclarence, looking highly perturbed, made a hasty adieu, but out in the corridor, came face to face with his uncle.

"George, my boy! Bless me! What an unexpected pleasure!" The Regent patted the young man's arm. "What are you doing here? Inspecting your new step-mother? Well, that's why I've come! Is your father here? Take care of yourself, boy," and with another pat, His Highness shuffled off, much to George Fitzclarence's relief.

Passing Von Effa, the Regent motioned to his receding nephew. "Damned good soldier . . . but cuts a sorry figure with the womenfolk."

As he entered the salon, all the ladies sank into deep curtsies, eyes cast down. His Highness surveyed them with much amusement, finally selecting the Duchess as the first to raise. As he courteously greeted her, Adelaide took the opportunity to slightly lift her eyes, to look at the man, who from early childhood, she had been taught to regard as an ogre of iniquity.

Thick, swollen legs, garbed in white, tight-fitting breeches, were straddled apart in an ungainly position. He was now raising her, her eyes traveling up to his gross, obese body in its pale-blue jacket, the gold buttons almost stretched to bursting point; to his neck in its multiple folds of neckerchief, forcing his head into an unnatural backward position. He wore a neat, brown wig, but his heavily painted and powdered face was like some half-hideous, half-comical mask.

Now he was kissing her hand, then her cheek and welcoming her to England. The charm of his voice astounded her; it was a voice that could send a woman's senses reeling . . . to momentarily forget his massive appearance.

"Your bridegroom seems somewhat reluctant, Ma'am. I expected to find him here. Have no fear . . . I'll take him to task."

"I have no fear, Sir, otherwise I would not have left Meiningen."

Damnation. The creature with her plain face and nasal voice had spirit. Brother William looked like meeting his match. It should be interesting sport, watching the trend of events. When he spoke again, he was once more the charmer, even the Duchess being wooed into conversation.

After a short spate of polite talk, he took his departure, and the ladies, much relieved, begin to make preparations for retiring, when late as it was, the Duke of Clarence was announced.

"This is too much," bewailed the fatigued Duchess.

"After the introductions, you may retire, Mama . . ."

"And leave you alone? With your newly betrothed . . . ?"

"It would make it easier for me, Mama . . ."

"There is much I would discuss with him . . ."

"Not tonight, Mama. Besides, anything you wish to say should be said through the Freiherr . . ."

"I still do not think . . ."

"His Royal Highness, the Duke of Clarence." Even Von Konitz's voice held a note of weariness, as he announced the bridegroom.

As Adclaide made her obeisance, she had a brief glimpse of a short, stocky man, with a round, puckish face, topped by clusters of greying curls. Thankfully she noted he wore neither paint nor powder, his cheeks being naturally highly colored.

He raised her up, kissing both her cheeks and then, still holding her hands, smiled. "Welcome, Princess, and my apologies for not meeting you ere now." He suddenly laughed aloud. "I see you are wearing all my rings . . ."

"Yes, Sir. Are they not beautiful?" Releasing her hands, she held them up before her, slowly moving them around, so that the light from the chandeliers above caught the gleam of the jewels, splitting them into myriads of atoms of colored beauty.

He again took possession of her small hands, with their delicately tapered fingers.

"Yes, beautiful indeed. Beautiful little hands . . ."

She laughed. "I meant your rings. Vas a bride to be ever more spoiled? Five betrothal rings!"

"I did not know your taste in jewels . . ."

"I love them all . . ."

"Then you shall have many."

By now they were seated on one of the small settees, some distance away from the Duchess and her ladies, all of whom were having difficulty in keeping their eyes open.

Somehow there was no tension. Each found the other so much easier to talk to than either had anticipated. To William's thankfulness, Adelaide spoke good English, for he knew little German. There were so many things to talk about, but at last the Duke took his leave, happy and elated, highly satisfied with his bride-to-be, while Adelaide, for the first time since her betrothal, felt a new comfort stealing over her, a sense of well-being . . . an awareness that she was going to find happiness.

As the Duke and Duchess of Kent stepped ashore at Dover, there was a truly regal greeting awaiting them. The presence of His Royal Highness, Prince Leopold, who had come to meet his sister and her husband was enough to send the crowd into a frenzy of pity. Poor, poor man. The bride smiled and waved. A little on the plump side but pleasant, and oh so beautifully gowned. As for the Duke, well, the menfolk who had served under him in the army couldn't be blamed if they added a few boos to the general cheering.

Then in the carriages provided by Leopold, they drove through the flag-bedecked town, out and away to *Claremont; Claremont* in all its summer beauty which had been placed at the disposal of the newly-weds for as long as they wished; the master of the house going abroad for an indefinite period.

Much to the disappointment of the Regent, who loved to entertain, there was no grand ball or state dinner on the eve of the double wedding. It was the Queen who settled the matter. Her health was too poor for her to participate and both bridegrooms being so heavily in debt, it would only serve to anger the people. Moreover, she insisted, after the wedding both parties must go and live in Germany for a while, until some of their debts had been settled.

Now in the drawing-room of Kew Palace, illuminated by the brilliant afternoon sunshine, William awaited the entry of his bride. Only members of the Royal Family—apart from the officiating clergy and the Earl of Liverpool—were present. He had wanted to bring along his two eldest children, George and Sophia, both of whom Adelaide had met and liked, but no, his mother had been adamant. It would be an insult to the house of Saxe-Meiningen.

When Adelaide frankly stated that she intended to be a real step-mother to his children, the Queen had been most critical. Impossible. Court society would be outraged, but Adelaide had stood her ground. They were not tiny children . . . she would be glad of their company. Unheard of! countered Her Majesty. It was her most fervent hope that it would not be long before Adelaide had children of her own. They, most definitely, could not mix with the Fitzclarences.

Adelaide, bless her, had just smiled her winsome, calm smile; his few days' acquaintance had already taught him that she had a will of her own. He wished now that he had not rented the house in Audley Square for his daughters; he could have saved that expense, knowing that when he and Adelaide took up residence at *Bushey,* the girl's would join them.

Now the double doors had opened and Adelaide on the arm of her mother, came towards him, to take her place before the altar that had been set up in the huge fire-place. Their eyes met; hers calm and trusting; his with pleasure as he noted how the wreath of diamonds sparkled around her soft, flaxen ringlets. Her dress of silver tissue and Brussels lace gave her small figure an almost ethereal look.

The Duchess of Kent, escorted by her brother, had already joined her husband, glittering and shimmering in gold and diamonds, casting haughty glances across at Adelaide. William eyed her scathingly. She would be a madam to handle, he mused. How fortunate he had been to find a bride so gentle and unassuming as Adelaide.

Now the Regent and the Queen made their entry; she, small, withered and aged, smirking with satisfaction that at last these sons of hers had toed the line and were taking wives; he, gross, full of gout, but oozing charm over his task of giving away the brides.

The Archbishop of Canterbury began to intone the wedding service and William, for once, was really listening. The Prelate was speaking to him now, "William Henry, wilt thou have this woman . . . wilt thou love her . . . in sickness and in health . . . forsaking all others . . ."

Dear God, yes. He intended to do all those things. He had seen too much of the chaos in his brothers' lives.

Clearly and loudly came his response, "I will," and then it was Adelaide's turn, causing a smile to play about William's mouth, as she whispered, "I vill."

Then they were kneeling on the crimson velvet cushions, and the Archbishop was pronouncing the blessing, "Those whom God hath joined together, let no man put asunder."

As they rose to their feet, William drew his bride to him, and gently kissed her on both cheeks. She was trembling. He spoke quietly. "There is nothing to be afraid of. It's all over now."

"I know, Villiam. I know. I am so happy. It makes me tremble."

He took her hand and led her to his mother and sisters. There was much kissing and tears from the spinster princesses, who had taken advantage of the occasion to bedeck themselves in new gowns and to air their diamonds. William felt a new sorrow for them. It had been damnable the way their father had kept them secluded, little knowing of the great tragedy it had brought to Sophia.

Footmen were being kept busy going the rounds with the decanters, the royal brothers, hot in their tight-fitting uniforms draining glass after glass and indulging in much hearty laughter.

Adelaide regarded her new in-laws with interest. She had already met the Duchess of Cambridge and was looking forward to being near neighbors when they all returned to Germany. What a queer little woman was the Duchess of York; so heavily painted, with her pale-blue eyes continually blinking as though to keep in time with her incessant chattering tongue. How small she was compared with the Duke's enormous height! He was the one now enjoying the telling of crude jokes, laughing loudly along with his audience . . . ladies and gentlemen alike.

She took a long look at the Duke of Kent and then a little smile of satisfaction played about her mouth. She was glad she had married William. He looked so much more friendly. The Duke of Kent might be younger but he was completely bald, fat and so pompous-looking. Moreover, stories of his cruel, sadistic military discipline had long since reached Meiningen.

They had dined and wined well but with what seemed almost indecent haste; the Kents were anxious to get back to *Claremont,* ordering their carriage, a gift from brother Leopold, to be brought round before seven o'clock.

William on the other hand was in no hurry to leave. Actually he was in a bit of a quandary having a mother-in-law on his hands. Neither the Queen nor the Regent had invited her to stay until her return to Meiningen, so nothing remained but to take her along with him and Adelaide to St. James's Palace, the only place they could go for their honeymoon.

He had at least managed one purchase . . . a new carriage, and their joint arms inscribed on the door panel announced their union, so after a final dish of tea with the Queen, they left for London, with the Duchess Eleanor sitting opposite.

By the time they reached St. James's the rain had begun to fall but this did not deter Adelaide from joining William on the balcony to wave to the crowd below. The palace had been illuminated and the lights caught both the glitter of diamonds and the gleam of raindrops, as the small silver-clad figure waved again and again.

When the Duke drew her in and ordered the window to be closed, the crowd refused to go away, yelling for Adelaide, and with smiling charm she again went out, happy that they should want to see her.

Then William, with husbandly consideration, insisted that she must come indoors. It had been an arduous, long, hot day.

Though it was the first day of their honeymoon, Adelaide and William had a busy day before them. As the Duchess Eleanor was returning home on the morrow they had decided to give her a farewell dinner party inviting all the members of the Royal Family. It therefore came as a blow to find the Duke's apartments so badly staffed; such a paucity of silver and plate. Hastily a messenger was despatched to *Bushey* to bring back the household silver, along with the butler and extra footmen.

Hardly had he left when a messenger, wild-eyed and dusty, arrived demanding to see the Duke. His son, Major George Fitzclarence had met with an accident. Driving from *Bushey* in his new tilbury the horse had bolted, throwing him and now with a broken leg, he was awaiting a surgeon at a nearby inn.

William did not hesitate. Borrowing the Regent's bed-carriage, and with hasty adieux to his wife and mother-in-law, he set off at once for the inn, causing the Duchess Eleanor to raise her hands in horror.

"Gott in Himmel! What is going to become of you, my daughter? His children still come before his newly-wed wife!"

When William returned, bringing George with him, Adelaide was all compassion.

Risking her mother's annoyance, she insisted on seeing her step-son who had the grace to be embarrassed.

"I'm sorry, Ma'am, that my father has brought me here, the day after your marriage . . . I must appear an interfering interloper . . ."

"Nonsense! You are velcome. Has everything been done for your comfort? Do not hesitate to ring for anything you vant."

"How can I thank you enough? My man-servant has been sent for. If I could stay here until . . ."

"You must stay here until you are fit to be moved . . ."

"You are very kind . . ."

As she left the room, she turned, smiling mischievously. "It's only in fairy stories that step-mothers are mean and cruel."

When, next morning, the Duchess Eleanor took leave of the newly-weds, neither mother nor daughter, with true German stolidity, showed any signs of emotion. Whatever tears they had to shed, had been shed in private. Smilingly, with William by her side, Adelaide gave her mother a final kiss, William, with hearty gusto, assuring her that it would not be long before they all met again.

In an effort to prevent his bride from moping, William ordered their carriage and took her sightseeing through the city and parks; but the enthusiasm of the few citizens who recognized them was lukewarm. Too well they could still remember the Duke's brusque dismissal of Mrs. Jordan. Pooh! they thought, what a poor exchange of women!

When they returned and found that Miss Sophia Fitzclarence was with her brother, William's spirits rose. He loved this eldest daughter of his and pressing her to stay for lunch, the conversation naturally turned to the well-being of the other children.

It was Adelaide who broached the invitation. Couldn't they all come to meet her the next day?

So soon? William was astounded but desirous of gratifying her every wish, he willingly acquiesced.

The boys were all away, either in the services or at school, but under the care of Sophia, now twenty-three, the girls, excited and curious about Papa's wife, now their step-mother, were thrilled with the invitation.

Because Amelia was only eleven, they came to an early dinner, William proudly introducing them one by one,

Adelaide embracing and kissing them as he did so. Well may he be proud, she thought, such beautiful girls. Please God, she prayed, give me equally beautiful daughters— and sons as handsome as George Fitzclarence.

3

Nowadays, they usually breakfasted in their bedroom, so that Adelaide could rest until mid-day, her time being very near. It didn't bother William that the other three newlywed duchesses were all expectant mothers; he was the eldest and it was his child that would be the heir apparent. Now it was more important than ever that Adelaide should take care, having in the last day or two developed a snuffling, sneezy cold.

"Stay in bed all day, my love," he suggested.

"No, Villiam, no. I do not vish to take to my bed until I must. Besides, I like to see to the ordering of my house . . ."

He patted her hand resting outside the coverlet, and when he spoke his voice was gruff with emotion.

"You . . . you've done marvels, Adelaide. Soon, we should be able to return to England . . ."

"That is vat I vant, Villiam. I vant our baby to be reared in England . . ."

They were interrupted by the entrance of one of Adelaide's ladies. "Ma'am. Sir. A messenger has just brought this note from the Duke of Cambridge."

"Ah!" William was already reading and then shouting with excitement. "Augusta is in labor! I must go immediately. I'm taking care there are no warming-pan changelings. I'm locking Augusta's door and sitting outside until the child is born."

"Really, Villiam, there is no need. Ve can trust Adolphus and Augusta."

"Can we? In an issue as important as this, can we trust anyone?" He bent and kissed her. "I must be away. Take care, my love. The shorter Augusta's labor, the sooner I'll be back."

He was out of the house and away to the stables to avoid wasting time sending round for the carriage. The Regent had been generous, allowing them eight horses and an extra carriage in addition to their own.

They had remained in England only three weeks, William's creditors becoming too pressing. With an allowance of 12,000 thalers a month, a cook and six footmen, the Clarences had set up house in Hanover. With free game, garden produce and wine, Adelaide, accustomed to frugal living had managed to budget within their means and for the first time in his life, William had incurred no further debts.

When in November, the Queen had died, hopes that his mother might have left him a legacy were quickly dashed, much to his chagrin. Adelaide, however, was full of genuine grief, having taken a liking to the lonely old woman, dying without seeing the grandchildren she had so long desired.

Left alone, Adelaide sank back gratefully into the feather bed. If William was going to be away all day, she might as well stay there. Her head ached and there was a painful tightness across her chest. She envied Augusta. Soon she would be holding her baby in her arms, while she still had several weeks to wait. She must persuade William that she was finding the constant traveling too much for her condition. After the snow and frosts of winter, the spring rain had come, transforming the hard, ridged and rutted roads into bogs of mud. She didn't know which made traveling the more uncomfortable, but William was so restless, always wanting to go visiting one relative or another.

She pulled the bell and asked her woman to bring her a drink. She felt hot and feverish and when the woman saw her mistress's flushed face, she immediately suggested that the doctor should be sent for.

Adelaide pooh-poohed the idea . . . at least not until the Duke's return, but when the short afternoon closed in, and darkness fell, and she began to find difficulty in breathing, she was only too glad to have the doctor if only for reassurance that all was well.

She was apologetic. "I wouldn't have sent for you . . . but the Duke is away. All I need is a James's Powder* . . ."

The doctor shook his head. "I'm afraid, Ma'am, your illness is more serious than you think. I shall have to bleed you."

Adelaide felt a stab of fear. She didn't want to be bled. Wasn't it excessive bleeding that had killed Princess Charlotte and her baby?

When William returned home, merry and talkative resulting from wetting his nephew's head too liberally, Adelaide was in a delirium. The shock quickly sobered him, but he, too, was alarmed at the bleeding. For three days he watched over her until on the third day, she had a miscarriage and their daughter was born only to live for six hours, the doctors blaming the attack of pleurisy.

Away at Amorbach, the Duke and Duchess of Kent, together with Charles and Feodora, were setting out for England. They were determined that their child, due in May, should be born in London.

When the time came for the christening of Prince George of Cambridge, Adelaide was up and about again, standing as godmother without any signs of jealousy or rancor, despite the news that the Kents now had a daughter and the Cumberlands a son, also christened George.

The courier from England had just arrived and William was going through his letters while Adelaide planned the day's menus. Suddenly he gave a guffaw of laughter.

---

* James's Powder, forerunner of the modern aspirin.

"Hark to this! A wedding invitation. Guess the bridegroom!"

She shook her head. "I know so few of your English friends . . ."

"But you know this one! My son George!"

"George! And his bride? Is she the lady to whom he has been devoted so long?"

William sighed. "Miss Scymour? No. There was no hope there. Before we left England, I told him to look elsewhere. He has reached an age where he needs his own establishment . . . and the lady will have a good dowry."

"Is she of good family?"

"Mary Wyndham? Yes . . . the daughter of the Earl of Egremont . . . but," he added with a note of embarrassment in his voice, ". . . not by marriage."

"Villiam, I vould like to accept the invitation. I vould like to go to England . . ."

"But, my love, we are not yet in a position . . ."

"Not if you accept the £6,000 offered by your government?" she asked quietly.

"You would have me humble myself?"

"Nothing vould please you more than to be at George's vedding . . ."

"By God, you are right . . ."

"And I," she whispered, "vish that my baby should be born in England . . ."

"You mean . . . ?" he asked incredulously.

She nodded. "Yes. I am vith child again . . ." She wasn't prepared for the way he rose from his chair, scattering his letters all over the floor, as he came and seated himself alongside her, taking both her hands. "By God, then, I will accept that £6,000 and they shall pay all the arrears. We'll refurnish *Bushey* and you'll see how your babies thrive!"

It was September and they had reached Dunkirk *en route* for England. The Regent had sent the *Royal Sovereign* to bring them to Dover, but before they could embark, Adelaide was taken ill, and suffered another miscarriage.

Despite her disappointment, she urged William that they should cross the Channel and so get home in time for George's wedding.

The weather couldn't have been worse, and by the time they reached Dover, Adelaide was so ill that she could go no further, and Lord Liverpool, hearing of their dilemma, offered them the hospitality of his house, *Walmer Castle*. There they stayed for several weeks, William never leaving Adelaide's side, but by November, they arrived in London and took up their abode at St. James's.

Their suite of rooms were just as they had left them after their brief honeymoon save that William had ordered their cleaning and airing.

As they looked around at the shabby furniture, the worn carpets and faded wallpaper, William put a reassuring arm around his wife.

" 'Tis only until the spring, my love. Then we will go to *Bushey*. There you shall have new furniture and you shall decide on the decoration . . ."

She nodded in agreement. "Ve shall have more money then. Besides," she went on gleefully, " 'twill soon be Christmas, and ve can have all the children here. Do you like Christmas, Villiam?"

Did he like Christmas? Nostalgic memories of Christmas, gone long ago, rose up before him. Memories of excited children, brilliantly decked Christmas trees, servants' balls, and most of all, his dear little Dorothy, his Little Pickle as the heart of it all. He mentally pulled himself back. "Like Christmas? By God, I do that. As you say, Adelaide, we'll have them all here, then before we know where we are, spring and *Bushey* will be on their way."

They had barely had time to unpack, much less arrange the rooms to their liking, when next afternoon callers were announced. "The Duke and Duchess of Kent." Nor were they alone, for following in their wake, came a nurse carrying the not yet six-month-old Princess Victoria.

Both William and Adelaide were overwhelmed by the

exuberance of the Duchess and the goodwill oozing from the usually reticent Duke as kisses were exchanged, but Adelaide had eyes only for the baby.

"How thoughtful of you to bring the Princess. May I see her?"

The Duchess of Kent motioned to the nurse who had remained in the background. "You will wait outside," and turning to Adelaide went on, "We are leaving London tomorrow. That is why we have called," but Adelaide was scarcely listening, having already taken the baby into her arms, her eyes alight with maternal love. William, not to be left out, was looking over her shoulder and remarking in his customary bluff manner, "She's a fat little lump."

"That, brother, is because she is healthy . . . properly fed . . ."

"I'm feeding her myself," interposed the Duchess archly. "Edward doesn't believe in wet nurses."

"Unhygienic! Unnatural . . . and unnecessary expense," ejaculated her husband.

Adelaide had seated herself, still holding the baby. "Pull the bell, Villiam, and order a dish of tea . . . and some refreshment for the nurse."

"You were saying," began William, "that you are leaving London?"

"Did you not know? Ah, of course, you have but just returned."

"We did hear rumors and stories about selling your house at Ealing."

Edward snorted angrily. "Damnation to the government. They had to interfere. I was asking £70,000 . . . it's worth much more . . . but there was no rush of buyers. So I decided on a lottery. There was a big demand for tickets . . . but then in stepped His Majesty's government, God damn their eyeballs."

Adelaide looked distressed. She was continually waging war against William's bad language but she could hardly raise a protest against her brother-in-law. William, however, looked amused. He was recalling the ostentatious household at Ealing; the bells at the gates to warn the household that callers were on the way; the little army of powdered flunkeys, and the gracious lady, Madame Julie St. Laurent.

"But why forsake Kensington? You are comfortable there?"

"Assuredly, but 'tis expensive living in London. We are renting this cottage at Sidmouth, where 'twill be much warmer and healthier for our daughter. We are taking but a small staff and Sir John Conroy as my equerry." He paused for a moment . . . "Apart from all other considerations, we find the proximity of the Regent most distasteful."

"Oh, come now. George can be a veritable tyrant we know, but do we have to let him interfere with our lives?"

"Have you not heard how he behaved at the christening of Victoria?" burst out the Duchess.

"I know there was some awkwardness . . ."

"Awkwardness! Sheer malignancy! Every name we suggested, he pooh-poohed, and there before the guests, including Tsar Alexander, he was most rude and sulky."

"Naturally I favored the child to be called Victoire, after her mother . . ."

". . . and I Alexandrina . . . or Elizabeth . . . or Georgiana . . . or even Augusta, after her aunt. There we were wrangling by the gold font, until the Archbishop, growing weary of it all, took matters into his own hands." The Duchess was becoming excited and voluble, but the Duke was content to let her tell the story, and having taken a deep breath she went on:

" 'Elizabeth,' said the Archbishop, coaxingly.

" 'On no account,' snapped the Regent.

" 'Charlotte?'

" 'Certainly not!' "

"Then," interrupted the Duke, drawing his wife to him. "Poor Victoire could stand no more and burst into tears."

Adelaide, hitherto silent, nodded in agreement. "No vonder! How dreadful."

"I think our brother then saw that he had gone too far

for he managed to mutter, 'Victoria then.' The Archbishop would have named her just that, but the Duke of York butted in with 'Alexandrina Victoria.' What should have been a most felicitous occasion was ruined . . . and he's been barely civil to us since."

Having exhausted the story of the christening, William sought a new line of conversation.

"I hear there has been more decorating and more building going on at the *Pavilion* . . ."

"Indeed yes. A new banqueting hall . . . a new music room, chandeliers in the form of great gilded dragons . . . expense no object, but not a guinea extra for us."

"Is Lady Hertford still reigning supreme?"

"Aye . . . and feathering her nest in no uncertain manner . . ."

"And our mutual friend Mrs. Fitzherbert?"

"Pestered to death. Her beloved Minney has at last found a man to whom she is partial . . ."

"The devil she has! And who is the fortunate man?"

"A certain Captain George Dawson, with little else but his army pay . . . and only a second son at that."

"Poor Maria. 'Tis understandable she is distressed. I wonder what the Regent now thinks about his darling Minney?"

The baby began to stir, but under Adelaide's gentle talk and swaying motions, she was soon lulled off to sleep again.

Victoire smirked facetiously. "What an excellent mother you would have made, dear Adelaide . . ."

William's eyebrows shot up. "Would have made? Will make. Once we are settled at *Bushey* . . ."

"You think Adelaide will be able to carry through her time . . . ?" came the sugary-sweet query.

"Of a certainty. The peace and calm of *Bushey* . . ."

"Ah yes . . . most of your . . . the Fitzclarence children were born there, were they not? Edward dear, much as I dislike to part you from your brother, 'tis almost time to feed the baby, so we should be on our way . . ."

Ill-natured bitch, thought William. They had only visited them to flaunt the child. He watched Adelaide as she gently surrendered the baby, wondering as to how she had taken the insult; marveling at her lack of any discernible hurt, pique or jealousy.

1820 was heralded in by bitter, cold, biting winds, even at Sidmouth, but they did not deter the Duke of Kent and his equerry, John Conroy, from taking long walks in the country. They were both big, healthy men, accustomed to standing up to the elements of the weather.

The Duchess was, therefore, much concerned when after one of these outings, Edward complained of feeling ill, but when the doctor cautiously prescribed calomel and a James's Powder, he laughingly waved it away.

In the morning, however, she was really alarmed when she noted his labored breathing. The hastily summoned doctor ordered leeches and it was Victoire herself who put them on her husband's temples. A second opinion was sought, and a doctor came racing down from London who prescribed extensive bleeding, taking a hundred and twenty ounces from the sick man.

Up in their nursery, Princess Feodora and Prince Charles knelt and prayed for their step-father. Stern, army disciplinarian he might have been, but during their short acquaintance they had come to love him.

Now the Duke of Sussex, Prince Leopold and Stockmar had arrived to give what help and comfort they could to the Duchess, who for five days and nights had scarce left his side. To her surprise, an affectionate message came from the Regent, which when repeated to the Duke, caused him to mutter, *"If I could only shake hands with him, I should die in peace."*

Die? He wasn't going to die, was he? Frantically, Victoire appealed to her brother, but he, along with Stockmar and Conroy, was busy drawing up the Duke's will, appointing the Duchess as sole guardian of their child and bequeathing his personal estates to his beloved wife and child.

With his last flicker of strength, Edward, Duke of Kent managed to scrawl his signature to the document. Speech was now difficult for him, but he was heard to be praying for the protection of his wife and daughter and for the forgiveness of his sins. Then with gathered strength, he fixed his eyes on Victoire and in an earnest, distinct voice, spoke. "Do not . . . do not forget me."

Victoire, Duchess of Kent was a widow for the second time.

While the preparations for the funeral of the Duke were still in progress, there came the news, only a week later, that the King was dead.

George, Prince of Wales, Regent of England was now George IV of England.

William looked up in surprise as his visitor was announced, but he was on his feet instantly to raise up the small figure in deep mourning.

"Madame Julie St. Laurent! This is indeed a pleasure, Ma'am." He led her to a chair and reached for the madeira. "For old times' sake, Julie, join me in a drink."

She took the proffered glass and regarded him as though searching for words. Then, "I am in London, Sir, on my way home to Canada . . . to my family. I have come to you, Sir, to ask a favor."

"Anything, that I can do, dear lady . . ."

"I . . . I would like to have returned to me . . . a number . . . quite a large number of letters that passed between the late Duke and myself. They were tied in bundles and were in a bureau . . . They all bore either his or my signature . . ."

"Say no more, dear lady. I will attend to the matter myself . . ."

"You do see, Sir, that I could not go personally to the Duchess . . ."

"No. Of course not. You were wise to come to me." Just how wise, she little knew, thought William. Victoire was in no mood to deal pleasantly with the Duke's late mistress. Every day since she had returned to Kensington, Adelaide had visited her, comforting her by spending long sessions praying aloud in German, for now, they were devoted friends. William, however, could not muster up any genuine affection for her even in her great sorrow. Now, to get these letters, he would have to accompany Adelaide on one of her daily visits.

"Where are you staying, Ma'am? As soon as I get the letters, I will have them delivered to you."

"How can I express my gratitude, Sir? I am staying at the convent in Ealing, with the Sisters of Compassion . . ."

William smiled at the mention of Ealing. Had Julie come for a last look, to take back memories across the Atlantic?

She rose and curtsied. "I will say a nova for you . . . and for your little Duchess . . ."

He bent low over her hand. "Thank you, Madame . . thank you."

When the footman at Kensington Palace admitted them, he informed them that Her Grace was in the nursery, but if they would wait in the library, he would announce their arrival.

"Not at all," was Adelaide's quick rejoinder. "I will go up and take charge of the Princess and so liberate the Duchess."

Left alone, William looked around the room. Like St. James's Palace, Kensington Palace was sadly in need of repair and redecoration. Perhaps now that his brother was king, something might be done.

He turned as Victoire swept into the room, looking pale and drawn. William did not kiss her; to have done so would have been hypocritical, but having courteously greeted her, he came straight to the point. "I had a visitor this morning. Madame Julie St. Laurent."

Victoire threw back her head with a haughty gesture.

"Should I know her?"

"I think you know of her."

"I do not wish to hear anything about her. Is this the time to mention her name to me . . . so soon . . . so soon after . . ." and to William's dismay she burst into tears.

"I am sorry to distress you, but the lady is leaving the

country as soon as possible and she asked me . . ." He fumbled as to how he should make his demand.

"Yes?"

"Among my late brother's possessions are bundles of letters, written by the Duke to Madame, and her letters to him . . ."

"Well?"

"The lady would like their return."

"That is an impossibility . . ."

"But why? Surely she has some claim . . ."

"I tell you it's impossible. I have already burned them."

"You have burned them! Without making any effort to return them . . ."

"Why should I? Why should I debase myself? In any case, I couldn't risk those letters being shown to anyone else . . . to have them repeated to my daughter at some future date . . . perhaps for some of them to fall into her hands . . ."

"Madame St. Laurent is an honorable lady. You would have had nothing to fear from her. Now she has nothing left."

"That is how I wanted it. She is entitled to nothing . . ."

William could stomach no more, without the risk of a violent scene with his sister-in-law.

"Please tell the Duchess I have returned to St. James's. She is at liberty to return in her own time . . . when you have both said a few more prayers. Good-day to you, Ma'am," and without the usual formalities, he angrily left the room.

"Drive round," he bawled at the waiting coachman. "Anywhere . . . out into the country . . . anywhere where the air is a bit sweeter than around here."

The man needed no second bidding. He was accustomed to His Highness' explosive outbursts. As the carriage moved off, William leaned back his head and closed his eyes. God Almighty! What wouldn't he give to tell that woman the truth but he had promised Edward, all those years ago, never to speak of the matter. Yet if he had stayed in that room a moment longer, he would have told her everything . . . that Edward and Julie were the parents of two sons, Robert and Jean, now young men in their mid-twenties. What kind of men had they become? It was so typical of his strait-laced, narrow-minded brother not to have had them acknowledged. Most damnable of all was that the elder boy, Robert, had been fostered by a certain Robert Wood, one-time personal servant to William while in the Royal Navy but settled in Quebec at the time of the boy's birth. That was how he, William, came to be in the secret. At the time, he had thought little of the matter, not being his affair, but when a year later, Mrs. Jordan presented him with their first child, his joy had known no bounds, rousing within him nothing but scorn for Edward's cold, callous behavior. Julie's mother, the Comtesse de Montgenet, had taken the second child which meant he did have a more gracious upbringing in keeping with his semi-royal birth, but the elder had to be content with the middle-class life within the means Edward allowed the ex-petty officer.

How he would like to see the expression on the Duchess' arrogant, plump face could he but tell her that Edward and Julie had been truly married! Morganatic, admittedly, but surprisingly, his mother, the late Queen, had entertained Julie on several occasions and both she and the princesses had thought her delightful!

A chuckle escaped him as he thought of baby Victoria . . . and her two grown-up step-brothers. Did the boys as yet, know of their true birth? Someday, someone would put the cat among the pigeons. He felt a sneaking longing that he should be around when it did happen. He wished no harm to his little niece but his bluff, down-to-earth honesty demanded that Julie's sons should have recognition such as he had given his children.

4

They made the move to *Bushey* earlier than anticipated for William now felt such strong antipathy against the Duchess of Kent that he avoided her company as much as possible. It wasn't only the affair of the St. Laurent letters but he felt the daily praying sessions were having a morbid effect on Adelaide; her conversation constantly veering round to the topic of "the end" which always resulted in William making coarse jokes and Adelaide weeping.

As they entered the house for the first time to take up residence, memories again stirred within him; no long line of servants as had greeted Mrs. Jordan. Just the necessary household staff as would be found in any country gentleman's house.

He had decided that their suite of rooms should be as far away as possible from those he had occupied with Dorothy, and now new furniture, chosen by Adelaide, had already been installed.

Bidding the Duchess to rest, and promising to show her over the house on his return, William went off with his agent to inspect the farm, but Adelaide had other ideas. She had heard so much of *Bushey;* knew so much of its former mistress . . . malicious gossip had seen to that . . . that she wanted to savor its atmosphere alone; to discover if there was really a promise of contentment to be gained, provided she could ignore the past.

Within a few days, much to her delight, William's daughters were returning here to *Bushey*. A house of this size needed the coming and going of young people. Sophia, her own age, would be excellent company. By now she had mastered the other girls' ages. Mary was twenty-two; Elizabeth nineteen and Augusta seventeen. Why was

Sophia still unmarried? She was good-looking, clever and charming, as indeed they all were. William said she had had several excellent proposals, but the minx had turned them all down. It would be so entrancing to watch these girls being courted, betrothed and married, just as if they were her own daughters. As for thirteen-year-old Amelia, still petted and cosseted by her father, well, it was good to have one daughter left who was still a child.

Slowly, unattended, she went down the broad staircase, curious to see what lay beyond the heavy doors. The first room she entered was obviously the dining-room, with its long polished mahogany table and heavy sideboard laden with silver dishes, epergnes and tureens. What in the name of Heaven was that huge, bulky contraption making passage round the foot of the table so constricting? She pulled the bell and when the footman appeared, she pointed and bluntly asked, "Vat is that?"

The footman cleared his throat. "That, Your Grace, is the foremast of the *Victory* . . . the ship on which Lord Nelson was killed."

"Ah . . ." The monosyllable was of complete acceptance. Many times she had listened to William's stories of his friendship with the famous admiral and knew of his grief. If this was William's memorial to his friend, it must remain. With a wave of her hand, she dismissed the man and went to inspect the mast more closely. She gazed at it in wrapped thought. This husband of hers might be blunt-spoken; often coarse and hasty-tempered, but he had one outstanding quality . . . love and loyalty for his friends and family. Had he any real love for her, she pondered, beyond concern that she should give him an heir? For her part, she felt a gentle, warm affection for him, knowing that as royal husbands went, she had indeed been fortunate.

She went across the marble-paved hall into the room opposite. As she had guessed, it was the main drawing-room, large and spacious, with three big windows facing on to the garden, but as she slowly looked around, so her dismay grew. This room was sadly in need of redecoration. The damask coverings of the chairs and settees were drab and faded as were the drapes. The carpet was thin and threadbare and the wallpaper gave no hint as to its original color, except over the mantelpiece, where a picture had been removed, leaving a startling, glaring square of riotous color.

Again she pulled the bell and when the lackey entered, she turned on him almost violently, pointing to the empty space on the wall. "That picture! Vy has it been removed?"

"It was the Duke's orders, Your Grace . . ."

"Then I give the order that it has to be put back at once . . ."

"Craving pardon, Your Grace, but the Duke was most insistent that it was removed before . . ."

"Before I came. I know. Now I am telling you to put it back. I vill vait until it is done."

The man looked helplessly at the little, sandy-haired woman giving her orders with such determination. God! They would have to watch their step with her around, but the next moment he was speeding down to the kitchen for a step-ladder, and bidding one of the others to go up to the attic and retrieve the heavy gilt-framed portrait.

In the meantime, Adelaide sat waiting patiently looking out across the lawns. Along the borders there was a gay profusion of spring flowers, giving promise of the beauty to come, when the rose-beds now sending out fresh green shoots, reached the peak of their glory.

She had not long to wait. Two men came carrying a large oil-painting, while another mounted the step-ladder and between them, the portrait was put back in its place. Not a word was spoken and it wasn't until the double doors had closed that she rose from her chair and went over to the mantelpiece.

She gazed up at the smiling face, so skillfully portrayed by the artist. So this was Dorothy Jordan. Time and again, she had been instructed, with sly innuendoes as to her own serious countenance; that Mrs. Jordan's greatest charm was in her delightful smile and laughter. Now she could feel its compelling captivation, lifting her heart, easing away all hostile feeling; all jealousy. She smiled back, and behind the smile, she renewed her inward vow, to take to her heart all William's children . . . this woman's children.

It wasn't until after they had dined that William suggested they look round the house.

As she had anticipated, he exploded in wrath, pulling the bell violently when he saw that the portrait was still on the wall.

"By God! I'll have the whole lot of them thrown out into the road. I gave the order that . . ."

Adelaide put a restraining hand on his arm "Listen, Villiam. They are not to blame . . ."

"I gave the order to have that portrait removed. I will not have you distressed . . ."

By now a footman had answered the bell, but Adelaide had the situation in hand as turning to him she said firmly, "You are not needed. You may go."

She faced back to William, a gentleness in her voice. "I am not distressed, Villiam, but your daughters might have been, to find their mother banished to the attics . . ."

"They do not count. You come first . . ."

"But it is a beautiful portrait of a beautiful voman. It gives so much joy to this room."

He looked at her in perplexity, shaking his head. "You amaze me, Adelaide. First you give your love to my children. Now you show no objection to having the portrait of their mother gazing down on you, day by day . . ."

"Vy should I? I vas but a child when she vas mistress here. You must have loved her, Villiam, to remain together all those years."

He was lost for words, but standing by her side he clumsily took her hand, kissed it, and rested it against his cheek, murmuring, "You are more than I deserve, Adelaide. I am indeed a fortunate man."

Adelaide was supremely happy. *Bushey* had fulfilled all William's and her step-children's praises. Rooms had been redecorated; new furniture bought, but only to a strict budget, bills being paid immediately upon presentation. The gardens were Adelaide's greatest joy, as each day throughout the early summer, arm in arm with William, they walked among the flower-beds, planning and scheming. She was quite content to remain at home, while William went up to town to visit his brothers or friends, but he never stayed away overnight.

Returning from one of these visits, he burst in upon her, shouting excitedly, "What do you think, Adelaide? We're going to be grandparents! George's wife is with child."

She looked up from her embroidery, smiling, "You are indeed elated, Villiam. I shall enjoy being a grandmother, but ..."

He took her hand. "I know, my love. I shouldn't have been so clumsy ..."

"Vat I vas going to say, Villiam, vas that I shall enjoy still more being a mother." As he looked into her radiant face, the realization of that enigmatic smile dawned upon him.

"Adelaide, do you mean ...? Oh, my love ... when?"

"Early in February. Vhen does George become a father?"

"October ... oh, I'm pleased for him, but now, Adelaide, I can think of nothing but our baby." He held her close. "Nothing must go wrong this time. I'm glad we're here at *Bushey* away from all the strife ... glad that your sister Ida is coming to stay with you. Her visit will help to pass the waiting months away ..."

Ida, Duchess of Saxe-Weimar, wasn't the only German princess to cross the Channel in the summer of 1820. A far more tempestuous lady, bent on asserting her rights, landed at Dover; none other than Caroline of Brunswick, determined to be crowned Queen of England.

George had tried to keep her out of the country, offering her a large income to stay away and when she indignantly refused, had taken her name from out of the Prayer Book.

Despite the widespread knowledge of her scandalous behavior on the Continent, there was considerable support and sympathy for her; so much that the country was split into two parties.

Now the King wanted a divorce. There was ample evidence of adultery against her. Caroline was to be put on trial, but damn the confounded woman, it meant cancelling the coronation, for which he and his new mistress, Lady Conyngham, had been making such wondrous preparations.

The consternation of the Royal Family and the aristocracy grew. Would there be a revolution? The unrest throughout the country was steadily mounting. One false step and the smouldering disquiet could burst into flames.

The Duke of York was most concerned. If the King was to obtain a divorce, remarry and beget an heir, he would never succeed to the throne. Accordingly he threatened to be one of Caroline's chief supporters unless George promised not to remarry, but before any satisfactory promise could be made, the Duke of York found himself a widower, the Duchess dying early in August. Now his prospects were brighter than ever. He could remarry and beget an heir; the Elector of Hesse, quickly offering his daughter as the new Duchess. The Duke, however, was in no immediate hurry, being too much at the moment under the influence of his mistress, the Duchess of Rutland.

Adelaide, contentedly entertaining her sister at *Bushey,* proving to her that William was no ogre, but a gentle loving husband, suddenly knew fear. Not so much that she would meet the same fate as Marie Antoinette, as Ida had long ago prophesied, but that all their hopes and aspirations should prove fruitless.

Moreover, as William's sisters were quick to point out, with the passing of the Duchess of York, she was, after them, the first lady of the land, and must take more part in public functions. This, they advised, would mean dressing on a much more lavish scale, but what really pestered Adelaide was that they must spend more time in London—

back to the draughty, dingy apartments at St. James's, for the government insisted that the baby should be born in London.

Another lady who felt she had grounds to be afraid was Maria Fitzherbert. If the truth of her secret marriage was dragged out, what would happen to her? Accordingly, with her elder adopted daughter, Minney Seymour, they went over to France on a protracted holiday.

At the end of October, George Fitzclarence presented William and Adelaide with their first grandchild, a daughter, who was to be named Adelaide. Would the Duchess be godmother? Adelaide was delighted, but would George please do something for her? His naughty little minx of a sister, Elizabeth, had jilted dear Captain Fox, after she had taken such pains to maneuver the match. Would he speak to her? She would take no notice of her or of her papa.

George stammered and stuttered and tried to make excuses for Elizabeth. Truth to tell, he was in her confidence. She was now no longer partial to the gallant captain, having met the Earl of Errol, whose estate was so much more noble, apart from all his other refinements. Moreover, he had it on the best authority, that the Earl intended asking the Duke for Elizabeth's hand. Had they better not wait events?

It was almost like a royal wedding. That at least was the verdict of the crowds watching and waiting outside St. George's, Hanover Square, on the cold December day when Elizabeth Fitzclarence was married to the Earl of Errol. Accompanying the Duke and Duchess of Clarence, was Princess Sophia, who, along with Princess Augusta, had insisted on providing the bride's wedding gown. As the royal carriages drove away from the church of St. James's for the wedding breakfast, there were resounding cheers for all the members of the family. Adelaide was content. These young girls were fortunate that they could make their choice.

She felt so much more light-hearted these days, since Caroline had been acquitted. The risk of revolution or civil war had been eased. She had a loving family around her . . . and soon she would have her baby.

The Christmas season was almost upon them. She would have to take things quietly, her time being so near, but that was no reason why the others shouldn't have their customary festivities.

Now with the wedding over, she could proceed with her plans for entertaining but she had grown to such a monstrous size, that getting about was difficult and uncomfortable. In vain did William try to persuade her to rest more.

"No, Villiam. Exercise is necessary for an easy birth." But when that night the pains began, she was filled with alarm. William did his best to hide his own fear of another miscarriage, staying with her throughout her long labor, comforting and encouraging.

On December 10th, a bulletin was issued. *Her Royal Highness is as well as can be expected. The infant is born before its time about six weeks.*

It was a girl weighing eleven pounds, remarkably like William. For several days, Adelaide, worn out, was scarcely conscious of what was going on, while William, anxious and terrified of what might be the outcome, hardly ever left her side, but there came the day when another bulletin was issued, happy to be able to state that the Duchess of Clarence and her infant were doing very well.

Now William could give vent to his joy and relief when on the first day, Adelaide was allowed to sit up and nurse her baby.

"The most wondrous sight in the world," he said tremulously, holding and frequently kissing Adelaide's hand. He caressed the baby's plentiful golden hair. "They say she's like me. God forbid."

"If she takes after your sisters, Villiam, she vill be beautiful . . ."

"But she will have a very different upbringing. I will

see to that. Royal she may be, but I will not have her cooped up and restrained . . ."

"Events vill vork themselves out, Villiam, but now I am so happy. So very, very happy. At last I have my baby here in my arms. Our baby, Villiam."

He knelt by the bedside, still holding her hand, his head bent low. His voice came muffled. "I was so afraid, my love . . . so afraid . . ."

"God is good," she whispered back. "I prayed so hard that he vould spare this baby . . ."

She could feel his tears on her hand. "I, too, prayed . . . but not for the baby . . . for you, my love . . . when the doctor grew alarmed . . . I knew that life without you would be a torment. Oh, Adelaide, Adelaide, that it should have taken me so long to tell you that I love you . . . truly love you."

She gripped his hand still tighter. "And I, Villiam, love you. I began to love you that very first time ve met. All this time I thought . . . I thought, that our marriage vas to you . . . just a necessary convenience . . . nothing more."

He rose to his feet, and bending over her took her in his arms, kissing her tenderly. "My dear, dear little wife . . . I never expected to hear you say that . . . to me . . . old . . . bad tempered . . ."

"Nonsense. Now you are young again . . . vith a baby to dangle on your knee." She looked at the sleeping child. "God has indeed been good."

They had a wonderful Christmas, Adelaide being up, and though only a looker on, thoroughly enjoying herself. Then no sooner was Christmas over than the christening took place. This time there was no argument about the child's name, the King specially requesting that she should be called Elizabeth Georgiana Adelaide, which naturally served to fill the Duchess of Kent with fury, not merely about the name, but that her child now ranked below the new princess, and that Adelaide's royal presence was so much in demand.

William, of course, gloated over the Duchess' discomfiture, but Adelaide was quick to take him to task.

"There is nothing certain, Villiam, that our child vill ever sit upon the throne. If the King gets his divorce, he might marry. The Duke of York is contemplating remarrying. For my part, I do not care. I have no regal ambitions for my child. I am so happy to have a child . . . a child to love . . . who in return will love us . . . I am quite content, Villiam."

March had truly come in like a lion; violent winds howling round the battlements of St. James's, rattling the rain-lashed windows like a giant trying to gain entrance. It had been a hard, bitter winter, consequently Princess Elizabeth had enjoyed few outings in her baby cart, much to her mother's regret, for both she and William were firm believers in fresh air as against hot, stuffy rooms. Soon, however, they would be returning to *Bushey,* for with the better weather and better road conditions, the journey to and from London could easily be accomplished when necessary for state duties.

The baby was a healthy little creature but Adelaide longed for her to have the fresh air of the countryside; to see her take her first steps on the *Bushey* lawns; to watch her grow up as an ordinary little girl, not as a possible future Queen of England. It was therefore with some alarm that visiting the nursery, she found the baby screaming and kicking out her legs, as the nurse gently massaged her abdomen.

" 'Tis nothing, Your Grace," volunteered the nurse, noticing the Duchess' apprehension. "The Princess has as yet had no bowel movement today . . ."

"But surely she should not be screaming like that." She took the baby in her arms, caressing the unhappy little bundle. "There, there, my *liebchen.* You're with Mama now. Don't cry, my little *liebchen.*"

But the baby continued to cry so much that William, looking for Adelaide, joined her in the nursery.

"Give her to me," he blustered confidently. "I'll soon quiet her. Now then, what ails Papa's little girl? What a noise! When you screw up your face like that you truly do look like your queer old papa," but when even his experienced handling failed to soothe, he handed her back to the nurse, saying that perhaps they had better have the doctor to look at her, although he didn't expect it was any more than bellyache and wind.

That was exactly the doctor's diagnosis. Just a bit of constipation. He prescribed a gentle laxative. Nothing to worry about. She would soon be herself again.

The little creature, however, did not respond to the physic; in fact it seemed to increase the pain, judging by the violent kicking and screaming. Neither would she take food. For three days Adelaide hardly left the nursery. Sometimes the baby, exhausted with pain, screaming and hunger, would doze fitfully only to awaken for another bout of screaming.

The doctors . . . a second opinion had been called in . . . still persisted that it was nothing more than stubborn constipation, now prescribing opium and sulphur.

William argued with them. After considerable experience in childish ailments, he had never come across its equal, but on the third night, the Princess having fallen into what appeared to be a deep, natural sleep, he persuaded Adelaide to go to bed.

It was about midnight when her woman roused her. The baby was worse.

Hastily throwing a loose robe over her night-gown, Adelaide, followed by William in night-shirt and sleeping-cap, dashed up to the nursery. The nurse was attempting to soothe the screaming child whose lips and mouth had now taken on a purple hue. Adelaide almost snatched the child from her. "Vat is happening? Vy is she blue?"

"It is convulsions, Ma'am. Brought about by the pain . . ."

"Vell, do something. Oh, Villiam. Vat can ve do? Vat can ve do?"

A nursemaid was already filling a bath with hot water, and having put in a liberal handful of mustard, the nurse approached Adelaide.

"A hot bath will give her relief, Ma'am. 'Tis the established treatment for convulsions . . ."

Half reluctantly, Adelaide handed back the baby, going down on her knees as the tiny body was lowered into the water. Silently she watched. Silently she prayed. The strident screaming subsided to a gentle sobbing pucutated by long, indrawing breathing.

"There! What did I tell you?" triumphed the nurse. "A few minutes longer, then I'll take her out."

When the nurse, with warm towels lifted the child on to her knee, Adelaide moved to take her, but she felt William's restraining arm. Together, with arms around each other, they stood and watched. Then, piercing the silence, the baby gave a scream, more shrill than ever, kicking out its limbs in violent contortion, and as the screams grew still louder, so the once beautiful face became contorted with pain.

Now Adelaide was screaming. "My baby! My baby! Give her to me! But before the nurse could obey, the screaming ceased and a gentle gurgle came from the agonized body, a whisper of a sigh, and then silence once again as Adelaide fainted in William's arms.

Escorted by a squadron of 10th Hussars, the tiny, embalmed body of Princess Elizabeth Georgiana Adelaide, was laid to rest at Windsor by the side of Princess Charlotte's baby son.

The Duchess of Kent, putting aside her dislike of William, came to sympathize, but William knew that keep down she was gloating. Victoria was once again in leading position.

The coronation was now to be held in July, and Adelaide would have to play her part in the round of festivities, balls and assemblies, no matter how near her heart was to breaking. Her mother's teaching had been so thorough, that she knew, being royal, she must never betray her feelings. Yet William recognized that something must be done to ease her pain.

"How would it be, my love, to have two of your sister's

children stay with us for the summer? Just think how they would flourish at *Bushey!*"

It was a good idea. She was longing to hold a child in her arms again . . . even another woman's child was better than none.

No sooner had they discussed it than William dashed over to Ghent, and thanks to the favorable impression he had made on the Duchess of Weimar, was allowed to bring back with him, Lou-Lou and Wilhelm, two of her children.

By the time the May blossom scented the lanes to *Bushey,* Adelaide was able to attend another wedding . . . that of Frederick Fitzclarence to Lady Augusta Boyle . . . again the smiling, loving step-mother.

5

Today, the Fitzclarence family were all gathering at St. James's Palace, ostensibly to watch the departure of the Duke and Duchess of Clarence on their way to the coronation, but at the same time all determined to rail at Papa over his failure to get tickets for them to attend.

"It is too, too devastating," Sophia's voice was full of petulance, "especially when you consider that my younger sister, Elizabeth, is there, flaunting herself . . ."

"Well then, you should have accepted the hand of one of your many aristocratic suitors," began Augusta.

"That's enough from you, Miss. I shall marry when I'm ready, not before. I wonder what can be keeping George?"

"His wife. Probably she doesn't want to come and won't let him come," giggled fourteen-year-old Amelia. "They're always quarreling . . . I've heard them."

"La, haven't little pitchers got big ears? I shall take care not to invite you to my establishment . . ."

They were interrupted by the double doors being opened to admit William and Adelaide in their ducal robes.

The girls curtsied prettily but Amelia could not contain her admiration. "Oh, Papa, doesn't Aunt Adelaide look beautiful . . . oh so very beautiful?"

William affectionately drew his youngest daughter to his side. "You're right, sweetheart, she does indeed." He glanced down at the slight figure. "See! You make us all feel very proud." His eyebrows lifted. "George not here yet?"

Almost as he spoke, they heard quick steps in the hall, and without waiting to be announced, Colonel George Fitzclarence pushed past the footmen.

"Tremendous doings in the city, Sir! The Princess Caroline has been to Westminster demanding admission . . . and been refused." He was breathing heavily, his voice full of excitement.

Adelaide blanched. "Oh no! Poor creature! Vith the King in his present mood, somebody should have advised her . . ."

"She was advised over and over again, but the damned stupid woman would heed no one. Now the day has been spoiled, before it's begun." There was a note of disappointment in William's voice.

"But that's not all. Finding the door closed against her, she drove on to the Banqueting Hall . . . and again she was refused admission. Somebody did open the door, just slightly . . . then slammed it in her face."

"Oh, the indignity of it all! That she, of royal blood . . . German blood, should be so insulted." Adelaide was almost in tears. "Vhere is she now, George?"

"Back at *Brandenburgh House,* I expect. The poor creature was assisted into her coach, screaming with rage, while the onlookers laughed and hooted."

"How could they be so cruel, when only a short while ago they were cheering her?"

"Ah . . . but then she was providing the spectacle.

Today it is my brother's turn . . . and a damned expensive turn it is." The Duke turned to George. "Do you know, his robes alone have cost £8,000? Yet here, we have to endure floors riddled with dry-rot, rattling, ill-fitting windows, and doors that won't close, all because His Majesty begrudges the pay of a carpenter."

"Then I expect it is true, Sir, that his hired jewels have cost but another mere £16,000. God! Uncle Nick should sparkle at that price!"

"George," remonstrated his step-mother gently, "You shouldn't speak so disrespectfully of His Majesty . . ."

He made a mock gesture of apology. "Dear lady, if you have a fault, it is that you are too royal . . . too dignified . . . but we love you in spite of it."

A clock on the mantelpiece chimed the hour. "Come, my dear, the carriage will be waiting." William offered his arm, and again the girls curtsied, as their parents prepared to leave the room.

George was still in a teasing mood. "Enjoy yourselves! And remember, Father, we insist that we have places at the next coronation . . . your coronation."

William paused. "Your Uncle Frederick, the Duke of York, comes next. In fact, he's already planning, declaring he's going to have just the same big show, and damn the expense . . ."

"Nevertheless, your turn will come, Papa, and then . . . I shall be Prince of Wales."

"George!" There was anger in his father's voice. "How many times have I told you that is foolish talk . . . dangerous talk. Have no more of it."

Behind his father's retreating back, George shrugged his shoulders. Then throwing himself into a chair, burst out, "It's damnable that neither I nor my brothers have any rank. All very well for you girls. You can marry into the peerage and so secure position, while we . . ."

"Have patience, George. If Papa ever does succeed to the throne, you know he will do something for you," consoled Sophia.

"Patience? I need more than patience. Mary is inconsolable that she is not to attend the coronation and is ranting and raving at me. I was glad to escape the house, I can tell you. Would to God I was a bachelor again!"

"See, George, Papa has given me tickets for the best stand. What do you say we all go . . . anything to chase away your fit of blue-devils."

"Please, please, dear George, do take us." It was fourteen-year-old Amelia pleading with her big brother. "We've all got new dresses for the occasion. 'Twould be dreadful if we could not wear them . . ."

The King was jubilant. No longer need he pester his brain as to how to obtain a divorce. Caroline was dead. He was a widower. Free to marry again. Free to beget an heir.

The news was brought to him as he waited at Holyhead, before sailing to Ireland. It was wonderful, marvelous news. When this Irish tour was completed, he would go over to Hanover. Perhaps his brother, Cambridge, could present some suitable princess worthy to be Queen of England, but by God, this time he was going to see her for himself, before opening any negotiations.

Spring had come round once again and out at *Bushey* the hedgerows were growing thick with new green shoots and the lush meadows were patterned with yellow buttercups and delicate mauve cuckoo flowers. Everything young. Everything growing according to Nature's plan. Please God, let this baby grow to full strength. Daily, Adelaide prayed but on April 8th, William had to write to the King, his brother.

It becomes my painful duty to inform Your Majesty that the amiable and excellent Duchess miscarried yesterday afternoon of twins. I want words to express my feelings at these repeated misfortunes to this beloved and superior woman. I am quite broken-hearted.

Last October, Elizabeth, Lady Errol, had presented them with another grand-daughter . . . another to be named Adelaide. The little newcomer was accorded a warm welcome, but it was for children of their own that they yearned ...

Another miscarriage and both William and Adelaide knew that the position was hopeless. They would never have a child, yet their marriage was far from being a failure. William had never known such tranquillity; never had his household been so well managed, free of debt. Under this influence, he himself had acquired a new dignity. His manners ... even his speech were more genteel.

For Adelaide's part, she had acquired a husband ... loving and generous ... a truly lovely country home ... and a ready-made family.

There had been more weddings; Mary had married Captain Fox, who had been jilted by Elizabeth, while Sophia had finally succumbed to the ardent wooing of Sir Philip Sydney.

There had been several trips home to Meiningen, and each time they had taken some of the children; Amelia, Augusta, Mary, and on two occasions, George had also accompanied them, glad to get away from his scolding wife.

They had gone over to Meiningen for the marriage of Adelaide's brother, Bernard. There, when her relatives exclaimed at the good looks and charming manners of the girls, she had preened herself as much as if she had been their true mama, and when William's sister, the Queen of Württemburg, remarked that she was quite unhappy that George was not of legitimate birth, she was in full agreement.

Then Ida had come to England and there, out at *Bushey,* her son, William Edward had been born. More grandchildren kept arriving, and it was Adelaide's delight to have them all together at *Bushey.*

Now there were just Augusta, Amelia, Adolphus and Augustus to marry. The two girls were especially dear to Adelaide, for they were so young when she had become their step-mother. She loved entertaining for them, but felt that she was considerably handicapped by the shabbiness of St. James's. She had brought *Bushey* up to near perfection. Now she was anxious to have an equally worthy home in London.

William listened patiently. Adelaide was right. His daughters deserved a better London residence, but by God, so did Adelaide. He didn't need much persuasion, and his letter was quickly in the hands of His Majesty's secretary.

His Majesty is fully aware of the inconvenience and unfitness of our present apartments here. They were arranged for me in 1809 when I was a bachelor . . . since when nothing has been done to them; and you well know the dirt and unfitness for the Duchess . . . I earnestly request for the sake of the amiable and excellent Duchess . . . you will represent to the King the wretched state and dirt of our apartments.

His Majesty must have been in a generous mood, for almost straightaway, he gave the order for the building of *Clarence House,* St. James's.

Whenever Adelaide held a party for the Fitzclarence grandchildren, she always invited Princess Victoria, for despite the friction between the Duchess of Kent and William, she had a deep affection for the child.

The invitation, however, was always declined. Now here was the Duchess being announced, quite unexpectedly.

Adelaide rose to greet her warmly, embracing and kissing her.

"Victoire! This is indeed an unexpected pleasure! Let me ring for a dish of tea, then you can tell me all the London news."

Victoire looked round Adelaide's cozily furnished drawing-room, with a sigh of envy. "How peaceful it is out here. How fortunate you are that you have no family problems . . ."

Adelaide laughed. "We have problems all the time. The girls falling in and out of love. The boys falling heavily into debt . . ."

"Ah, but they are not your problems . . . they're not your children . . ."

The protest died on Adelaide's lips as Victoire went on. "I've come to ask a favor. It's about Feodora . . ."

"Feodora?" There was both query and surprise in Adelaide's voice.

"Perhaps you have heard of the stupid rumors going around that the King is infatuated with her . . . intends to ask for her hand . . ."

"Oh no." Adelaide could not restrain the shocked horror. "He is too old . . . so gross . . . she is so young." She pulled herself together. "Not that I vish to be disloyal . . . if it is His Majesty's vish . . ."

"But it is not mine." Victoire almost spat out the words. "My daughter Victoria is going to sit on the throne . . . none other . . ."

"But His Majesty could marry elsewhere . . . then . . ."

"But it shall not be Feodora. I will not have her usurping her sister's birthright. That is why I am here to ask if Feodora might come to *Bushey* until I can make arrangements to send her to Germany to stay with my mother."

"You mean so that the King will have less opportunity to meet her?"

"Exactly. Last week he invited us all to visit him at Windsor . . . the first time since I was widowed. He was in his most charming mood, paying much attention to the stupid girl, who became enchanted with him."

"But surely not to the extent of . . . ?"

"Isn't the possibility of being Queen of England tempting enough for any girl? No, I'm taking no risks. When my brother Leopold goes over to Germany, she can travel with him, but in the meantime I'd be grateful if you would have her under your care."

"Of a certainty, Victoire. We shall be glad of her company."

William snorted with sarcasm when Adelaide reported the purpose of his sister-in-law's visit.

"How many times has she refused to allow Victoria to visit us? So afraid that my grandchildren will contaminate the little dear!" He chuckled. "We'll give Feodora the time of her life. Amelia and Augusta will adore having her. We'll have all the mob of grandchildren down . . . what do you say, Adelaide?"

Adelaide was quick to sense the change in Feodora. Formerly she had always been so shy, so self-retiring, quite content to be in charge of Victoria and to remain in the background while people bowed and fussed around her baby sister.

Now she was in a rebellious mood. " 'Tis good of you and Uncle William to have me here . . . but why? Since the King invited us to Windsor, Mama has behaved so queerly. 'Tis as though she doesn't wish me to meet anyone . . . for lots of gentlemen paid me great attention . . . and I did so enjoy it. And now I am to be sent to Germany."

Adelaide regarded Feodora with compassion. She knew Victoire was planning to get her married as soon as possible to some German prince, but Feodora at nineteen was much younger than most girls of her age. She had been kept so much in the background that she had grown up self-effacing, quite willing to pander to every wish of her baby sister.

"You will meet gentlemen at your grandmother's court . . . more than you meet here . . ."

"How I wish I had the same freedom as Augusta and Amelia, to choose or reject as I please . . ."

"But, Feodora . . . you must never forget you are a Princess . . . Even an arranged marriage can be happy . . ."

"I don't want an arranged marriage. I want to marry for

love. I suppose you heard about Lieutenant-Colonel d'Este . . . ?"

"Your mama did mention the incident . . ."

"I never thought Mama would refuse her consent . . . He is the son of the Duke of Sussex . . ."

"But . . . but he is . . . was born of a morganatic marriage."

"He gave me two rings," she went on, her voice low as she recalled the joy, "but Mama was furious . . . I have never seen him since . . ."

"You will love again, *liebchen,* never fear, and Uncle William and I will be there at your wedding for we adore going to weddings . . ."

It was incredible. The Duke of York was dead. He, William, Duke of Clarence, was now heir-presumptive to the English throne.

Whatever grief he felt was soon forgotten as Parliament, realizing that his elevation meant more entertaining, decided to raise his allowance by £3,000 a year and to give Adelaide £6,000 a year. Moreover, he must be given some position of note, so having served in the Navy, it was decided to revive for him the office of Lord High Admiral of England.

With regret, Adelaide left *Bushey,* to take up residence in Whitehall, and here, she entertained on the occasion of Augusta Fitzclarence's marriage to the Honorable John Kennedy-Erskine.

She was now expected to entertain on a much more lavish scale than she had done at *Bushey.* There, her guests had consisted mainly of the Royal Family, William's children and their families. Now she was confronted by government officials and their nose-in-the-air wives and naval officers of all ranks. She faced each banquet with dread, feeling awkward . . . feeling that she was being criticized, but it was her duty, and duty for Adelaide always came first.

This was to be a very private, intimate dinner. Just the six of them . . . Amelia going to dine with the Kennedy-Erskines.

Adelaide was glowing with satisfaction. Everything had gone the way she had planned. She had written her cousin—several times removed—Prince Ernest of Hohenlohe-Langenburg, suggesting that he call on the Dowager Duchess Augusta of Saxe-Coburg. There he would meet the Princess Feodora . . . a very charming girl of nineteen. Ernest, a major in the Hanoverian army, and fond of feminine company, lost no time, and being much taken with Feodora's good looks and quiet manners, wrote accordingly to Adelaide.

Then followed a spate of letters between Adelaide, the Dowager, the Duchess of Kent, Prince Leopold and the prospective bridegroom himself. Feodora was not consulted. Even when she returned to England, she was still in ignorance of what was going on, much less that her dowry of £4,000 and yearly income of £400 had already been fixed.

Now Prince Ernest had arrived as William's and Adelaide's guest, and tonight, Feodora, along with her mother and Uncle Leopold, were coming to dinner.

It was oh, such a dignified dinner party. The conversation was stilted for it was such an important occasion, no one must speak out of place. For once, William and the Duchess of Kent were managing to refrain from wrangling, while Prince Leopold was as silent and taciturn as usual.

Leaving the gentlemen to their wine, Adelaide led the way to her drawing-room.

Victoire was quick to open the conversation. "A most amiable young man, Adelaide, do you not think?"

"Indeed I do . . . but more important, what does the Princess think of him?"

Jerked out of her thoughts, Feodora spoke impulsively. "When I first met him at Amorbach, I couldn't help thinking how like Augustus d'Este . . ."

"Feodora! I thought you had forgotten him long ago . . ."

"Oh, I have, Mama . . . but Prince Ernest is just the same age . . . thirtyish . . . an army officer . . ."

"And there the likeness ends," snapped her mother. "Now you must sing for Aunt Adelaide . . . and I will play."

Obediently, Feodora moved over to the piano and as she passed Adelaide, she said mischievously, "But, dear Aunt Adelaide . . . this kinsman of yours is far more handsome than Augustus d'Este."

Prince Ernest was entertained at Kensington Palace and at *Claremont*. He took the Princess Feodora driving. Then three days after the meeting at Aunt Adelaide's, the betrothal was announced.

Now followed such a week's entertainment, as Feodora had never known. It seemed that all the entertainment that should have been hers as a young princess was being rolled into one mammoth affair to be the first . . . and the last. She was, however, rapturously happy. Despite their short acquaintance, she was in love with Ernest and he with her. Listening to the bells of Kensington Church pealing out their joyous message, she thanked God for her good fortune on this her wedding day.

The bridal procession was drawn up and waiting in an ante-room. She took her place at the head of it, lovely in her gown of virginal Buckingham lace, the only note of sophistication being the splendid diamond necklace, glittering at her throat . . . His Majesty's wedding gift. The bridesmaids, Princess Victoria and Princess Carolath, cousin of Aunt Adelaide, both feeling very grown up in their long lace gowns and white satin slippers, were beginning to get fidgety, anxious for the next step in this exciting event. As the mantelpiece clock struck three musical chimes, Feodora slowly led the procession into the Grand Hall, to join the King who had so particularly requested that he should be allowed to give her away, only to find that he had not yet arrived.

In the Cupola Room where the marriage was to take place, heavy with the fragrance of spring flowers, Prince Ernest, along with Dr. Kuper of the Royal German Chapel, awaited his bride. She was late, but was not that her privilege? Slowly the minutes ticked by. The bells ceased to ring. What was holding up the bridal procession?

The Duchess of Kent could hardly contain herself. She guessed that the King had failed to arrive. After a whispered conversation with Adelaide, who in turn whispered to the Duke, she gave a sigh of relief as she saw William leave the chapel.

As he reached the hall, Feodora, standing there looking distraught and anxious, broke away to meet him. "Oh, Uncle William . . ."

"It's all right, Feodora. The King has not been able to come, so I wondered . . . May I take his place and have the honor of giving you away?"

"Oh, Uncle William. Dear Uncle William." Throwing aside all decorum, she put her arms around him, kissing him tenderly. "There is no one I would like better. What would I do without you and Aunt Adelaide?"

She took his arm, while Lehzen fussed around, once again arranging her train.

What had happened to the King? There were those who had seen him that day and knew that he was not ill. At the reception, there were sly innuendoes as to His Majesty's non-appearance. Did it hurt too much, they asked, to see the delectable Feodora married to a handsome young prince?

William, in his new high office and enjoying his increased income, felt the time had come to entertain his mother-in-law in a more lavish manner than on the last occasion she had visited England . . . the time when she had brought Adelaide to be his bride.

Adelaide was delighted at his thoughtfulness and the pleasure of entertaining her mother. To celebrate the Battle of Waterloo, a Venetian Regatta was held on the Thames, which was followed by a sea trip from London to Plymouth and back again, so that when the Duchess Eleanora returned to Meiningen, she was bursting to extol the excellency of her son-in-law.

Unfortunately, several of the Lord High Admiral's high-handed movements caused great displeasure to His

Majesty and the government, resulting in William being asked to resign his office.

Back at *Bushey,* William sat and brooded. For the first time since his marriage, his depression became so great, almost bordering on insanity, that Adelaide found herself with another problem . . . how to keep the Duke's condition from public knowledge. Again her stiff Teutonic training, her royal upbringing stood her in good stead. She was a most loyal, considerate wife, waiting on and tending him herself so that the servants could but guess, and under her quiet, gentle influence, it was not long before he was his usual jolly, happy-go-lucky self.

Amelia Fitzclarence walked disconsolately through the shrubbery. She wanted to get away from the house . . . away from where Aunt Adelaide could see her and come to comfort her. She didn't want comforting . . . at least not by Aunt Adelaide . . . only her dear Horace. It was so cruel of Papa . . . Why couldn't he understand her loneliness? All her sisters married . . . all her brothers away . . . even dear Augustus. It had been stupid of Papa to allow Aunt Adelaide to persuade him to enter the Church. He hated the thought of it . . . but he had succumbed to her persuasion . . . odd the power she had in persuading people to her way of thinking. She stopped. Perhaps she could persuade Papa to allow her to marry Horace! Quickly she retraced her steps, entering her step-mother's drawing-room by the french window.

Adelaide welcomed her with a smile. "Come and sit vith me, Mely. Here is your needlevork. I grieve to see you in the mops."

"I do not intend to glump, but then it is so devastatingly lonely, with Augustus gone . . . and now that Papa refuses to allow me to marry Mr. Seymour . . . Couldn't you, dear Aunt Adelaide, talk him round?"

"But it vould be a disastrous marriage, Mely. He is a vidower, with several children . . ."

"When Papa married you, he had more children than Horace . . ."

"So he had . . . but most of them vere grown up . . . In any case Mr. Seymour cannot afford a second marriage . . . having settled all his money on his children . . ."

"But I love him, Aunt Adelaide . . . and he loves me. What does money matter?"

"Vould you vish to see your sisters living in comfort . . . vhile you lived in poverty?"

"Papa would give me some money . . ."

"Perhaps that is vat Mr. Seymour hopes. Your papa has already spoken to Lord Hertford, but he refuses to assist Mr. Seymour."

"Why is everyone so cruel? Do you know, Papa insists that I return all his love-letters . . . all that I have left to remember him by. Won't you talk to him, dear Aunt Adelaide?"

"I have talked to him, Mely, but he vill not listen . . . and he is right. This gentleman is not suitable . . . there vill be others," but Amelia was no longer listening, dashing from the room to hide the threatening flood of tears.

Up in the *Bushey* nursery, various Fitzclarence grandchildren slept, including the youngest one—recently born to Sophia . . . another Adelaide!

In the schoolroom, Prince George of Cambridge and Princess Louise of Saxe-Weimar vied with each other as to who could do the better hand, while not to be outdone, Louise's six-year-old brother, Edward, struggled away with his letters.

With the french windows of the drawing-room wide open, Adelaide and William dozed the June afternoon away, lulled by the drone of insects and the heady perfume of massed roses.

The sound of carriage wheels caused them both to sit upright, Adelaide patting her curls into position, while William stretched and yawned.

" 'Twill most likely be Victoire," began Adelaide.

Now William was wide awake. "Then if it's that old cow . . . I'm going. I'll pay a visit to the piggery. I prefer the old sow to her."

"Villiam . . . you shock me . . . you hurt me . . ."

He looked back before going out of the window, "And I can guess what she's come to gibble-gabble about . . ."

He was gone, for now the footman was announcing the Duchess of Kent.

Adelaide greeted her warmly, then pulled the bell, ordering a dish of tea. Victoire, as usual, was most becomingly gowned in a pastel blue muslin, overwrapped with an excessive number of lace flounces. The tiny pagoda parasol she carried, was of the same material while her wide leghorn straw hat, boasted nothing but simple yellow ribbon trimming.

"I hardly expected callers on such a hot afternoon," began Adelaide.

"I simply had to come . . . to talk to someone . . . who would listen. Really, I am the most pestered of women . . ."

"Victoria? Is she not vell?"

"Victoria is always well. She is a healthy child . . . save for her temper. Her fits or tantrums still continue . . . even now that she is ten. I feel good whippings are the only cure . . . but Lehzen spoils the child. Do you advocate whipping, Adelaide?"

Adelaide was slow to answer. "No . . . I don't think so . . ."

"La, it was stupid of me to ask you. Unless you have a child of your own, you cannot imagine how they provoke you . . ."

"The Princess Feodora? Ven is it she expects her child?" came the patient interruption.

"October. Ah, I wonder when we shall see the dear child again? I do indeed miss her, for she had more control over Victoria than anyone. But that isn't what I came to talk about. I suppose you have heard the gossip about my brother, Leopold."

"That he has taken a new mistress? But surely that is no concern of anyone else . . . ?"

"Is it not? Not when he plans to marry her?"

"But such a marriage vould not be . . . it vould merely be morganatic. So vy the concern?"

"The creature is an actress . . . Caroline Bauer . . . a German actress . . . a cousin of Stockmar . . ."

Adelaide laughed. "I still do not see the cause for concern. Stockmar is Leopold's dearest friend . . . it all sounds like a truly family affair . . ."

"But I will not meet the creature. Why cannot he be content with a mistress discreetly housed, to be visited occasionally, or better still why doesn't he marry a princess and live a normal life again? She's using blackmail to force him into marriage, threatening to return home to Germany if he does not. Poor, poor Leopold. I have tried to reason with him . . . tried to advise him."

Caroline Bauer looked round her boudoir, with a yearning question in her eyes. Today was her wedding-day, but would her bridegroom, Prince Leopold, be spending his bridal night with her? The pretty room with its walls draped in pink silk; the adjoining bathroom . . . the first she had ever had . . . had long since lost the excitement they had inspired on her arrival two months ago.

She thought back to the memorable day when he had called on her after seeing her performance in a musical comedy, professing to having fallen in love with her, she being the reincarnation of his late wife, the Princess Charlotte of England. Would she be his morganatic wife?

She did not need much wooing. There was the promise of a beautiful home in England, a generous allowance and the devotion of a prince.

The villa in Regent's Park that he had taken for her was all as he had promised, but there was no anxious lover awaiting her, nor did he materialize until the second day. Then there was not a single kiss . . . not even a handshake, just a tall, melancholy-looking man, who when he did manage to speak, was to complain that she had allowed herself to become sun-burnt.

He had returned the next day, requesting that she should play the piano for him. From piano-playing they had progressed to Caroline reading aloud, while he drizzled.

That was two months ago; two months of piano-playing, German novels, and drizzling. She didn't know which she hated most. Perhaps the horrible tortoise-shell drizzling box. There the Prince would sit, feeding it with silver buttons and metal threads from uniform froggings and epaulettes. Then his finger would keep the little wheel turning z-z-z-z, reducing the metal to dust. He was, he said, hoping to get enough silver to make a soup-tureen for his niece, the Princess Victoria. Damn the soup-tureen! Damn everything and everybody! She could stand it no longer, and accordingly issued her ultimatum. Either he kept his promise to marry her, or she returned to Germany.

To her surprise, he had capitulated almost immediately, and now she was feverishly awaiting his arrival. He had promised to bring witnesses . . . that he would have a marriage contract drawn up . . . that all would be well.

It was well into the evening before he arrived, but from her bedroom window she noted that he was accompanied by another gentleman. So he intended to keep his word this time!

Slowly she went downstairs, wearing a white lace gown, and a rose in her hair . . . her only ornament. At the foot of the stairs, her mother awaited her and on her arm, entered the big garden salon . . . beautiful with its profusion of flowering plants.

They both curtsied to the waiting Prince, he bowing low in response. He took her hand and led her to the table where various documents were laid out, bidding her to sign, here, here and here. Leopold put his signature. So did Frau Bauer. So did the gentleman.

The wedding ceremony was over. There had been no blessing from the Church, but she was now Countess Montgomery, with a settled income. She looked at Leopold. He was actually smiling . . . and his melancholy dark eyes seemed to be alight for the first time.

With the gentleman's departure, Frau Bauer took her cue, saying that she would see to the arrangements for a meal, Leopold never before having eaten at the villa.

Offering his arm, he and Caroline walked out into the garden, now in July at its very best.

"I am sorry, *liebchen,* that I have been so tardy . . . but . . ."

"I understand, Sir. Having lost the woman you loved . . . it was a hard decision to marry again . . ."

"But now I have got her back. You are Charlotte. I will teach you all the little ways that endeared her to me . . . beginning tonight." There in the cool silence of the summer evening, he kissed her passionately, and Caroline, hungry for his love, returned the caress with abandonment.

It was the last day of the year; and it seemed as if the cold, raw fog was deliberately blotting out all that had happened during the past twelve months. Countess Montgomery and her mother stared round the drawing-room of the house that Leopold had taken for them, situated near *Claremont.* The carpet and curtains were faded beyond all hope of recognizing their original colors; the chairs and sofas were old-fashioned and uncomfortable.

Leopold had been a devoted lover-husband for exactly four weeks. They had sung duets together, played billiards; walked in the country lanes, hand in hand. Then it was all over. He must go over to the Continent, but he would meet her in Paris. She had been in Paris exactly four months before he arrived . . . then he took rooms in another hotel. They were back on the original footing . . . drizzle-box and readings, Leopold daily complaining of his ill-health.

He had only stayed a week or two before returning to England, telling her that he would send for her as soon as he found another villa, this time, he hoped, nearer to *Claremont.*

So this was it! Caroline was furious. There wasn't even a proper kitchen . . . no cooking utensils.

When Leopold called that afternoon, footmen brought cooked meals, which was to be the daily arrangement, while other footmen carried a bundle of new German novels . . . and the drizzle-box.

Her only hope of freedom was Cousin Stockmar's whispered intelligence, that the crown of Greece was being offered to his master . . . then she would be free to return to Germany.

It was obvious that the King could not live much longer. He would not allow anyone to see him apart from his doctors, his valets and the Marchioness of Conyngham . . . nor would he allow housemaids to enter his room . . . so conscious had he become of his gross figure and unprepossessing appearance. His gout gave him excessive pain . . . he often had as many as eighteen leeches on his knees . . . pain that caused him to be bad-tempered and irate.

Since the death of the Duke of York, William had made up his mind that seeing he had no child to inherit the throne, he would sit upon it himself; and accordingly listened to Adelaide's advice, becoming more temperate in eating and drinking and going to bed at an early hour.

He must live, otherwise Victoria would come to the throne; and not yet being of age, a regency would have to be set up. Already rumors were going around. Leopold had refused the throne of Greece. He would rather be Regent of England. So would his sister, the Duchess of Kent, backed by her comptroller, Sir John Conroy. And when on the throne, damn it, he swore he'd stay there until Victoria came of age . . . he wouldn't be able to rest in his vault if he thought those Coburgs were in power.

6

William was out in the garden earlier than ever that morning. He had slept but little, having visited George the previous afternoon, and noticed his deteriorating condition. It wouldn't be long now, and even as he bent to pluck a perished rose that the gardener had missed, he saw the carriage coming up the chestnut drive.

It was Sir Henry Halford . . . the King's physician. William went back to the terrace to meet him, knowing full well the reason of his visit. As Sir Henry rose from making his obeisance, William joked, "Well, how about telling Her Majesty? She dreads the thought of being Queen. I prefer that you inform her . . . I don't wish to upset her, on this day of all days."

When Adelaide entered the breakfast-room, it was obvious she had been weeping, having heard the arrival of the coach, and knowing its portent. Sir Henry, with his best bedside manner, kissed her hand, assuring her of the love and allegiance of the country.

The tears then became uncontrollable as she put into his hand the prayer book she was carrying.

"Take this, Sir, to mark the day ven she, who never expected such high elevation, became consort to His Majesty, Villiam IV."

Before breakfast was over, the coaches were rolling up, bringing one Fitzclarence family after another. There were kisses and congratulations, mixed with the constant flow of Adelaide's tears. Up to the nursery went the babies and the nurses while their excited parents passed round the decanters, drinking to the health of their darling papa, now King of England. Who would have thought of it in their childhood days? If any of them spared a thought for their mother, Dorothy Jordan, none spoke of her.

Only one daughter was missing; Augusta, who was expecting a baby, but she sent her love with the message to her dearest papa, that if it was a boy, she was naming him William.

With the arrival of the Duke of Wellington, William got down to the serious business of drafting out his declaration, reading it to first one and then another, receiving much varied advice as to his elocution. Even his valet, Jemmett, had to listen as he got his master into his admiral's uniform for his first Privy Council at St. James's.

It was good that the next day was Sunday. After all the excitement of yesterday, William needed a day of rest. According to his weekly habit, he and Adelaide attended church. The preacher, for this very special Sunday, the first of his reign, was his son Augustus, newly appointed the Rector of Mapledurham.

Adelaide now saw her opportunity for righting a certain matter that had long pestered her sensitive mind. Wasn't it too ridiculous that certain royal brothers should be at cross purposes, one with the other? Before the day was out she had persuaded William to be friendly with Ernest, Duke of Cumberland, and that the latter gentleman and the Duke of Sussex should be reconciled.

. . . and before the day was out, the news came that Augusta Kennedy-Erskine had been delivered of a . . . daughter. Not to be outdone of naming her after Papa, the baby was to be named Wilhelmina . . . and again the same request . . . would Adelaide be godmother?

So Leopold had refused the Greek throne! Caroline was almost in despair . . . Leopold was becoming a greater bore each time he called. How she longed to go back to Germany to pick up the threads of her acting career! Thank God, he had business in London for a few days. She much preferred her own company. She had now been here in the *Claremont* cottage for six months, six months of absolute misery.

It came to her that here was a chance to look over *Claremont*, Leopold never having invited her to do so. She went up the stone steps into the black and white marble hall. Over a screen, a hat and shawl hung, dusty and rotting. Surely . . . surely they couldn't belong to . . . to Charlotte? It was thirteen years since . . .

A raucous squawk startled her. It came from a cage in the corner of the hall. Going over to it, she was confronted by an emaciated parrot, clotted with dirt and obviously verminous. Had it, too, belonged to Charlotte?

She had no wish to see any more of the house. The atmosphere was depressing to an extreme.

Out once again in the garden, blinking her eyes in the sunshine, she was surprised to see a little girl coming towards her, astride a pony. A dog ran alongside the laughing child, whose golden curls bobbed up and down in the breeze. When she saw Caroline, she drew the pony to a standstill, stared, then with a shake of the reins wheeled around and galloped away.

Caroline resumed her walking, but within a few minutes pony and rider were again approaching, this time with a short, plump, arrogant-looking lady walking alongside. When they were within a few yards of her, they came to a standstill, eyeing her with undisguised disdain and contempt. Caroline could feel her color rising, but she dare not speak, now knowing them to be the Duchess of Kent and Princess Victoria. With a final shrug of scorn, the Duchess turned the pony, and they all moved away.

Tears of rage were mounting within Caroline. That Leopold, who professed that she was the reincarnation of Charlotte, should show no desire to present her to his sister was bad enough, but that she should be treated with such arrant scorn . . . it was not to be borne.

By the time Leopold called on her again, most of her boxes were packed and down in the hall.

"What is the meaning of this?" he demanded peremptorily.

"Just what your eyes can see, Sir! My boxes packed ready for departure."

"But you cannot leave me, Caroline. I rely on you. You are so essential for my well-being . . ."

His arms went around her. "Caroline, *liebchen,* can't you understand? My heart died the day that Charlotte died. I'm like what I am, because of that. Give me another chance, *liebchen.*"

"What? Just to tide you over . . . to entertain you until you decide which throne you want? I know now that when you sent for me to come to England, you were negotiating for the Greek throne . . . That was why you delayed the marriage . . . hoping it would not be necessary . . ." She could go on no longer, bursting into tears.

"It's not true, *liebchen*. I need you. I truly need you . . ."

"Only when the mood takes you. You have held me like a state prisoner. I have wasted two years of my life . . . reading to you . . . listening to your incessant drizzling. You are a miserable . . . self-opinionated bore . . ."

His mood suddenly changed. "Very well then. You are tired of me . . . unfaithful to your promises . . . 'Tis you who are false. When do you propose to leave?"

"I have taken accommodation in a London hotel . . . until I arrange my passage . . ." She hesitated. "There is one thing I would ask you, Sir. May I take the parrot with me? He needs looking after . . . he looks so dejected . . ."

"Take Coco? By all means. I shall be glad to be rid of the pestilential bird. This then is farewell." He pulled the bell, ordering the footman to carry his drizzle-box back to his waiting carriage.

As Leopold had greeted her on arrival without a kiss or handshake, so he departed from her life.

There was all the ceremony and pomp customary to the funeral of a king . . . but few people mourned George IV with any sincerity . . . except perhaps Maria Fitzherbert. She could remember the handsome, charming prince who had wooed her with such ardor, persuading her into a secret marriage. Now William had told her the marriage could be made public, and as proof of its legality, she could put her servants into mourning—and into royal livery . . . and she should be created a duchess. She had declined the latter. She had risen above all the humiliations George had heaped upon her . . . loving him to the end. She saw neither triumph nor satisfaction in a coronet, but she was grateful for William and Adelaide's friendship.

Once George had been laid to rest in the Royal Chapel, William lost no time in taking up residence at Windsor, much to Adelaide's sorrow at leaving *Bushey*.

No sooner had she crossed the threshold, than she stopped and sniffed suspiciously.

"Vat is this horrible smell?"

"Gas, my love. The latest invention for lighting . . ."

"It is horrible . . . It makes me feel ill. Cannot anything be done about it?"

William shrugged. "We can have it taken out . . . and go back to candles and lamps . . ."

"I vould like that much better. Please give the orders, Villiam."

William, too, had ideas for certain alterations. Out must go all his brother's French chefs. He wanted good, plain English food. Out must go George's German band. He could soon organize an English band, and it wouldn't cost him £18,000 a year . . . and Hell and damnation, he certainly did not want that collection of wild animals. A public zoo had recently been opened at Regent's Park. They were welcome to them all, free of charge.

Another matter. Why shouldn't the people be allowed to see where their king and queen lived? Straightaway, he gave orders that the terraces should be open to the public.

Wherever he went, he was acclaimed with enthusiasm. He took to walking about London incognito, but he was always eventually recognized, soon to have a mob around him. Adelaide protested. It was not the correct behavior of a king. He took the censure well. Adelaide was always so right.

There were official functions, state occasions and everlasting reviews, Adelaide always accompanying him lest he should overstep the mark and make himself look ridiculous.

He had been shaken to find that George had left thousands of documents unsigned . . . now his task. Accordingly every night, after dinner, he tackled the job; Adelaide by his side, with a bowl of hot water and a towel. When his fingers went into cramp, she bathed them with loving tenderness.

Now came the most difficult task of all . . . to choose their household staff. While at *Bushey,* few of those near the throne had visited them, yet now they were toadying for high places. Adelaide and William had already settled the matter; they were for members of the family and the few real friends they possessed. Lord Errol, Elizabeth Fitzclarence's husband, was appointed Adelaide's Master of Horse, while Mary's husband, Colonel Fox, became her equerry. Ladies and women of the bedchamber were chosen from relatives and friends of William's sons- and daughters-in-law.

To be her Chamberlain, Adelaide elected Richard, Earl Howe, good-looking, in his mid-thirties, married with several children. In the whole household, there was only one German: Dr. Küper, whom she appointed as her Chaplain.

They had come to Brighton. This gorgeous, exotic palace was his. He had called on Nelson's widow, taking Adelaide with him, laughing and joking as he recalled the day he was best man at her wedding, at the same time noting, a worthy little woman no doubt—but as he had seen all those years ago . . . so very colorless.

Maria Fitzherbert was also in residence; her house being but a stone's throw from the Pavilion. They had called, giving her an invitation to Court, and the reassurance that her allowance of £6,000 a year was being continued.

All London society followed them to the resort. His sister Augusta took a house nearby. The Fitzclarences were there in full force, all determined not to miss out on anything; not to allow one to get more than another.

George was being difficult. He wanted to be made a peer, with a regular allowance. William retorted that, as yet, he could not do it; whereupon the whole family became truculent, George resigning his office of Deputy Adjutant General. Then Adolphus, Groom of the Robes, and Frederick, his father's first equerry, together with sons-in-law Sir Philip Sydney, the Honorable Kennedy-Erskine and Colonel Fox, all equerries, followed suit.

Adelaide was greatly distressed; the more so because she knew that William had done his utmost for his children. What should have been a pleasant rest and relaxation, became a daily torment of continuous bickering.

They were back in town by October for the opening of Parliament. There was a murmur spreading among the working people, that now King Billy was on the throne, they could expect better things. The long-needed reform was in sight. Wasn't the King a man of the people? A man who could see their needs? Better wages. Better working conditions. More houses. More employment. Yes. King Billy would see that the Reform Bill went through.

Adelaide, while sympathetic with the poor and energetic in work to alleviate their appalling living conditions, was dead against any reform. Give them more money, she argued, and you give them power and with power they would rise up against all authority. There would be a revolution.

Prime Minister Wellington was in full agreement with her, and his announcement that the Tory Government was opposed to reform, was the signal for outbursts of violence up and down the country, and serious riots in London.

Adelaide and William now lived at *Clarence House,* and it was there, as they were dressing for the Lord Mayor's banquet, that William had a caller. It was Wellington.

"I crave your pardon, Sir, for this untimely intrusion, but I have come to warn you that the crowds are in a very ugly mood tonight . . ."

"Bah! Who is afraid of a crowd of layabouts . . . ?"

"I am thinking of the Queen, Sir . . ."

"She is never afraid . . . but . . ." Here His Majesty gave a sly wink, "it's your blood they're really after."

"Yes, Sir . . . I am well aware of that . . ."

"Well, then, that's easily settled. You shall ride in our carriage . . ."

"Craving your pardon, Sir, it is worse than you think. The mobs are out of hand . . . they intend to cut off the gas lighting . . . A November night is ever murky enough . . . but without any kind of lighting . . ."

William was silent for a moment. Then, "What do you suggest?"

"That I ask the Lord Mayor to postpone the banquet . . ."

"But that would show us to be chicken-hearted cravens . . . we should be the laughing stock of London . . ."

"Better that, than . . ."

Adelaide had now joined them. She listened attentively. "I am not afraid to go . . . light or no light . . . but an attack on us could spark off the . . ."

William knew what she was going to say and halted her.

"You're right, my love. The banquet is cancelled."

When Adolphus joined them, and learned the news, he was most put out.

"Papa! How could you? How could you let the Prime Minister persuade you to be such a muff? Now I owe £100 to my club. Everybody was betting as to whether you would or would not attend the banquet. I said you would . . . I was so sure of it . . ." He shrugged his shoulders. "The least you can do now, Papa, is to give me the £100 to pay my debt."

When later they met for dinner, the cancellation was the chief topic of conversation.

Lord Howe, seated by Adelaide, nodded in acquiescence. "You were wise, Your Majesty. There is no sense in inciting the mobs, and His Majesty, despite his courage, is not a young man."

She smiled back at him, grateful for his attention. No, William was no longer young. How wonderful it would have been had their ages been more equal . . . to have known him when he was virile and handsome . . . as was this man by her side.

7

The music-room of the Pavilion was packed with relatives and friends including a vast number of small children, all being held firmly by the hand to offset any unruly behavior that might mar the occasion.

The low hum of chatter died away as William, resplendent in admiral's uniform, entered with the bride on his arm, a look of fatherly pride emanating from his round, chubby face. True, he had shed a few tears in the privacy of his room. This was his youngest daughter, Amelia, the last to go from him.

As they took up their positions before the Bishop of Chichester and the bridegroom, Lord Falkland, William still had eyes only for the bride in her white lace gown. Thank God, he had done his duty by them all . . . the future of his daughters was now well assured . . . all had wealthy husbands, members of the peerage.

Now he looked across at Adelaide. Dear God, if only their daughter had lived. Instead, there was the Queen, with her sister's crippled child, Louise, and two of his nephews, George Cambridge and George Cumberland, loving them all as if they were her own, attending to their upbringing and education.

Now the ceremony was over and they were following the newly-weds into the banqueting hall with the great Chinese pictures on the walls, and the huge gilded dragons, supporting the myriad candle chandeliers, glaring down upon them. William gave the monsters a quick glance. He would have to do something about them; Adelaide was scared of them; afraid they were too heavy and someday would come crashing down.

The wining and the dining was soon under way. All Amelia's brothers and sisters were there, a wealth of silks and satins; a brilliance of military and naval uniforms, and elegantly dressed men.

It was a woman who tapped William on the arm with her fan. Later on, he never could recall her identity but she directed his gaze to a mirror, which not only reflected part of the banqueting hall, but part of the "deckers' room" where drinks were being decanted and trays of used crystal goblets washed with loving care. There, a footman, thinking himself away from all watching eyes, was pouring himself a drink, and quickly tossing it down his throat.

Without a second's hesitation, William confronted the wretched man as he was putting down the glass. For a moment, master and man stared at each other; then in a sarcastic voice, the King demanded:

"Is my claret to your taste, Sykes?"

"Sir . . . Sir . . ."

"For God's sake, man, say something. Don't just stand here."

Adelaide had joined him. "Villiam . . . not here . . . not today . . . Mely's vedding day . . . don't spoil it." She turned to the man. "You may go, Sykes. His Majesty vill see you in the morning."

As they watched him make his humiliated retreat, William good-naturedly remarked, "I thought it was damned funny . . ."

"But ve cannot have the servants taking such liberties. Vat vill you do vith him, Villiam? He is a married man, vith several children."

He drew her arm through his as they went back to their guests. "There's a vacant lodge at Windsor. I'll offer him a job as gate-keeper, but the others must be warned, any more sly-drinking . . . instant dismissal."

The mobs were getting out of hand, not only in London, but up and down the country. Arson was their chief weapon, hay-ricks, barns and out-buildings being set on fire where estate workers could not be spared to safeguard them, being needed to protect the country mansions, which all too often were the targets for gangs of ruffians and desperadoes.

In London itself, it was the young apprentices who stirred up the turbulence, whipping up the misery of the homeless and destitute into a frenzy of disorder and violence.

Since the fall of the Tory government, William had hoped for an improvement, but Adelaide felt only increased terror, aided and abetted by Lord Howe, himself a staunch Tory, dead against reform.

It was at *Clarence House,* as after dinner Adelaide and her ladies sat with their needlework and the gentlemen with their cards, that they heard the noise . . . the unmistakable noise of tramping feet and singing voices. When the tramping ceased and the singing became a confused hubbub of shouting and cursing they knew that the mob was outside their gate.

Somebody was giving orders; demanding silence. The subsiding noise was strangely eerie . . . unnerving. Then a clear-cut shout, "Come on out, Billy. Show yourself!"

William went over to the window and was about to pull back the drape, when Adelaide joined him. "No, Villiam, no. They vill kill you!"

"Scared to show yourself, Billy? Frightened of a few hungry men?" A stone hit the window, sending a shower of glass into the room.

William hesitated no longer. "The ladies . . . leave the room . . ." and drawing back the drape, flung open the window.

He stood there in the full light of the lamp-lit room, a little old, grey-haired man, facing the biggest mob he had ever seen, many carrying flaming torches and flambeaux.

"Reform! Reform! Reform!" came the chant from the hundreds of voices.

"Listen to me, my good men, it is up to the government . . ."

"You can direct them . . ." came back the answering shout.

"Send that ugly German frau back to her own country ... then you'll direct them!" The insult was a signal for a new chant, "Send her back! Send her back! Send her back!"

"She wears the trousers," came a laughing jeer. "Poor old Billy has to do as he is told." Now the jeering had grown to such a pitch that it was impossible for William to make himself heard or to discern the mob's catcalls.

Then someone was heard to shout, "Three cheers for His Majesty," and there the unpredictable crowd was giving one resounding cheer after another.

Still the King remained standing at the window. There were no further calls. The mob was now re-forming some semblance of procession and he could see they carried a tri-colored banner, bearing the words, "The Trades of London." As they began to move away, someone took up a song, and the sound of marching feet was submerged in the loud ebullient singing of "God Save the King."

Slowly William closed the window and as he turned to face the gentlemen, he found Adelaide at his side.

"You have been here all the time?"

"Yes, Villiam, it is my duty to be by your side."

He spoke to the assembly. "You had better join the ladies. Tell them all is well." He turned again to Adelaide. "I wish you had not stayed. You heard what they said?"

"I heard. Vy do they hate me so?"

"They know you to be against reform. Did you not write some days ago to Lord Howe, telling of your hope that the Tories would be returned to power?"

"I did ... but he vould not ..."

"He showed your letter to Wellington. That is how I know of it."

"But Vellington vould not repeat ..."

"Somehow there was a leakage. Oh, Adelaide, it is not safe to put your thoughts into writing."

"But you, Villiam, refuse to discuss vith me, this horrible reform business ..."

"And thank God for it, for I can thus truly say none of

your opinions influence me in any way whatever. Would to God I could make the people believe that."

The September day was cold and wet, but William and Adelaide on their way to Westminster glowed at the unexpected warmth of their reception. William had finally capitulated to Lord Grey's injunction that there must be a coronation. For a long time he had tried to sidestep the issue whenever the subject came up for discussion. He wanted no coronation. It was out of date. It was a waste of money. His argument was that with the people in their present mood, any extravagant spending would only stir up more anger, for the unrest was seething and bubbling all the time. He and Adelaide could never drive out in their carriage without being greeted with shouted insults, hissing and sometimes, showers of earth and stones.

The newspapers had taken up a rumor that Adelaide was trying to persuade the King to escape to Hanover, while pamphlets of foreign origin urged assassination and extermination of all royalty and the aristocracy. There were scurrilous lampoons showing Adelaide wearing trousers and William in petticoats.

Revolution was looming nearer, but Adelaide was of German royal blood. She might know fear, but she wouldn't show it. Instead, she went on quietly holding her drawing-rooms and assemblies. She might detest the word "reform" for the country, but she was industrious in her efforts to reform the Court.

She specially requested that the ladies should patronize English silk manufacturers and dressmakers, and that their décolletages should not be so indecently low, a request that threw many a fine lady into a pelter, believing that an ample show of bosom was her most attractive asset. Then she asked that they cut down on the number of feathers they wore in their hair. She herself never wore any, but when a lady, wearing any number from twelve to twenty huge feathers, bent to kiss her hand, she received the full force of their irritation in her face.

The same ladies, and their gentlemen, found Adelaide's balls and drawing-rooms incredibly dull. To be invited to dine with their majesties, was to them a penance; the King falling asleep as soon as the meal was over and the Queen working on her everlasting embroidery. What a frumpy, prudish Queen! What a bore, the King!

When she had chosen her household staff, she had endeavored to give posts to both husband and wife, so that they could be in attendance together, for her sensitive heart hated to part a married couple. There was a constant stream of marriages between her young maids-of-honor and gentlemen-about-court; weddings that William and Adelaide always attended; these newly-weds gradually building up a more decorous and dignified court.

As the coach moved slowly through the crowded streets William stole a look at his wife. God! She looked every inch a queen, in her dress of gold, and purple velvet train; diamonds in her hair and at her throat. He was glad that Grey had been so insistent. It was only right that the people should come out in their thousands to cheer their newly crowned king and queen; that they should be given a holiday with free feasting and drinking. The only qualm he still had, was that of being kissed by the bishops . . . he really loathed the idea.

It was a pity there had been so much discord about the arrangements. To begin with there had been the argument about Adelaide's crown. It had been suggested that she should wear that belonging to Mary of Modena. Adelaide was definite in her refusal. Then they would have to hire one. *"Gott in Himmel!"* What an indignity for a queen to be wearing a hired crown! She had a few jewels of her own; couldn't they be made into a coronet? What was more, she herself would pay the jeweler for his skill.

Then there had been the trouble with the Duchess of Kent, who had insisted Princess Victoria should walk immediately behind the King and Queen. William, however, was equally insistent that his brothers and sisters should take precedent over her. Consequently the Duchess had refused to attend or allow Victoria to be present.

For this coronation, all his children and their spouses were to be honored guests. Then George had brought him the news that several of the Tory peers were threatening to stay away, because there was no banquet, only a dinner for a hundred members of the Royal Family and that the whole affair was costing no more than a miserable £24,000. "What a cheap, shabby, *half-crownation.*"

Moreover, his wife Mary, wasn't feeling too well so she would not be able to attend.

She wouldn't, the contrary bitch, thought her father-in-law, but was quick to retort, "Tell them there will be more room for those who do attend . . . your lady-wife included."

Now as he strained himself in his tight-fitting admiral's uniform, he was wishing that last night's altercation could have been avoided. Frederick had visited him, making a final request that he and his other brothers should be given peerages, to rank equally with George, now Earl of Munster, Baron Tewkesbury.

"But George is my eldest son . . ."

"That should make no difference. Charles II gave dukedoms to all his natural children . . ."

"That, my son, was many years ago. Today's government would not consider the matter. God knows I had difficulty enough to secure a peerage for George."

"Surely, Sir, you can see the injustice of it. What have you offered us? The Order of Guelph! Bah! We should each be given an earldom."

They had argued and wrangled and Frederick had gone away cursing and disgruntled, leaving his father dejected, for Frederick was in charge of tomorrow's processional arrangements, and from what he had seen of the rehearsal, had made a good job of it. They were always bickering nowadays, both sons and daughters. No matter what he gave them, they were never satisfied. In addition to his peerage, George was a Privy Councillor and Governor of Windsor Castle. Adolphus had been given the command of the royal yacht. Frederick was Governor of the Tower, and their sister, Mary, now Lady Fox, was housekeeper of Windsor Castle. All the sons-in-law had been given royal appointments, and each and every one an increased personal allowance. When in March, Augusta Kennedy-Erskine had been widowed, she and her children had immediately taken up residence at Windsor.

Now as they stepped down from their coach, there were resounding cheers and shouts of, "Good Old Sailor King." William beamed in reply, but Adelaide looked pale and nervous, but managed a smile of gratitude as the King took her hand, and they began their walk up the aisle to the waiting bishops. As she listened to the solemn words, she became more in command of herself, while William was obviously ill at ease, especially when it came to performing the age-old rites.

As they left the Abbey, Adelaide held her head high. Come good or evil, she was now the crowned consort of the King of England. She felt strangely elated, as though the service had given her renewed dignity and courage to face all odds.

8

Adelaide had felt a deep sense of loss when she had to leave *Bushey* but when she learned that in the event of William's death it was to be one of her residences, the disappointment quickly receded.

Now as she rode through Windsor Park with Richard Howe at her side she realized that her love for Windsor was overtaking that for *Bushey*. There were miles and miles of grassy parkland, so ideal for riding, her favorite exercise. As they came to a bend in the road, it was to find several empty carriages and a number of grooms awaiting them.

Drawing in her rein, she smiled at her escort. "As

usual, I expect by now, most of my ladies are much fatigued."

"But not you, Your Majesty?"

She laughed. "I could ride on and on for miles vithout being tired. I have my father to thank for this accomplishment. He had me in the saddle at a very early age. Lady Howe? She does not care for riding?"

"No, Ma'am, no, but following your father's example, my small daughters have already begun their riding lessons."

"You are vise. They vill certainly be grateful in the years to come."

"If they ever look as beautiful and elegant in the saddle as you do, Ma'am, 'tis I who will be grateful."

Adelaide, her usually pale face already flushed with exercise and fresh air, felt her color rising still more.

"Flatterer," she countered, but she knew that in her black riding habit and tall hat, she did indeed look her best. William had many times praised her appearance, when she was leading off a riding party, but she could never persuade him to accompany them.

She smiled at the riders who had now joined them. "I am sorry if I have brought you too far. I did not realize the distance, but the carriages are here, and vill take you back to the Castle."

Dismounting, the gentlemen bowed low, while the ladies made small curtsies, only too pleased to be out of the saddle. Really! The Queen's energy was unsurpassable, but there were sneers and snide remarks as, having handed their reins to the waiting grooms, they packed themselves into the carriages.

" 'Tis noticeable, my Lord Howe is not fatigued . . ."

"If she thinks we are hoodwinked by her concern for our weary backsides, she is much mistaken . . ."

" 'Twould be a good gig if some of us were to follow them through the woods, where they walk . . ."

"But not before bidding the grooms take their horses by the wood skirtings . . ."

"Yet, Her Majesty is fond of walking . . ."

"La . . . I couldn't agree more . . . provided she is walking hand in hand with her dear Richard."

As the carriages bowled back to the Castle, Adelaide and Lord Howe were indeed walking through the woods; Adelaide holding her skirts high as they made their way, often through dense bracken, with Richard, every now and again putting a protecting arm around her small waist.

She turned to him. "Tell me, Richard, vat magic is there about a vood that makes one feel so young . . . so carefree?"

"Is that how you feel, Ma'am? Could it be the beauty . . . the peacefulness . . . the solitude?"

"But I am not alone. You are vith me . . ."

"Could it not be that . . . that we are alone together?"

His voice was low and seductive. Adelaide was quick to notice, and pointing to a cluster of shrubs laughingly remarked, "Look! There are others here . . . vatching us . . . Ve are trespassers. Did you not see that bush moving? Vat could it be? A fox? A badger?"

"No, Ma'am. I saw nothing. 'Tis your imagination. The animals sleep by day." There was a sulky note in his voice.

". . . as does my husband." Skillfully, Adelaide turned the conversation. "After a morning's vork vith his ministers, he is only too ready for his afternoon nap. This reform business is indeed causing him much agitation. He and I never speak of it now . . . that is vy, Richard, I appreciate your news and opinions of vat progress is being made . . . one vay or the other."

"The position is stalemate, Ma'am . . ."

"But surely . . . one side must break before long."

"All I can say, Ma'am, is God help us if the Reform Bill is ever passed . . . 'twill be the end of royalty and the nobility."

They had now reached the edge of the wood, where the grooms were waiting with their horses. As Richard helped Adelaide to mount, their eyes met, but she could only muster a troubled smile. The magic of the wood had been erased by the ugly word "reform."

Instead of ringing for her woman to help remove her riding-habit, Adelaide, reclining on a day-bed, thoughtfully sipped her tea.

She had long known that Richard had a certain affection for her, but deep down, she had hoped that he would never reveal it. Now, daily, she could sense the danger growing, for she was only too well aware of her regard for him. That William had never remarked upon their friendship was strange, for the scandal sheets frequently linked their names together . . . just as they linked the King's name, first with one of her maids and then another.

Perhaps William, though aware of her liking for Richard, trusted her. Yes, she did like him . . . but love, she had never before dared to think of. What would it be like to be loved by someone as young and handsome as Richard for now, even the pressure of his hand and his arm around her waist, set her heart racing in a way she could not comprehend.

A tap on the door brought her back to earth. It was a footman, announcing that Lord Howe wished to speak with her.

She felt a moment of panic. Had he come to make a declaration? She didn't want to see him. She was the consort of the King of England. She wanted no undignified affair.

"Tell him I vill see him later . . . that I am not dressed . . ."

The door closed. Would a clandestine love affair be so very wrong? It would be easy to cuckold William; he spent so much of his time dozing. There could be golden opportunities to be alone with Richard. Other queens had taken lovers . . .

There was another knock at the door. It was the footman, back again, with the message that Lord Howe must see her. The matter was urgent.

Great God! Had someone already started a scandal, before there was any truth in it? Buttoning up the jacket

of her habit, and attempting an air of coolness, she bade
the flunkey send him in.

She rose to receive him, and bending low, Richard
Howe kissed her hand. "Your Majesty, I have just been
in conversation with the King and Earl Grey . . ."

"Yes?" There was anxiety and bewilderment in her
voice.

"It would appear, Ma'am, that there are many who
resent our friendship . . ."

So she had been right. The gossip had begun in earnest.

". . . they blame you . . . for passing on to me . . . the
King's political confidences . . . and that I pass them on to
the opposition."

She almost laughed aloud with relief.

"But that is ridiculous! The King does not confide in
me . . ."

"You and I . . . and the King know that, but because I
fearlessly vote against reform . . ."

"You have the right to vote as you think . . ."

"Nevertheless, Earl Grey is below, demanding my dismissal, as your chamberlain . . ."

"Vat! How dare he! And vat does the King say?"

"He refuses, Ma'am, knowing that my duties are of a
domestic nature, assisting you in matters of English eti-
quette and custom . . ."

"Very vell, then, that is settled . . ."

"No, Ma'am, no. After discussion with His Majesty and
the Earl, I decided that rather than cause any faction, I
must resign." He held out the key of office.

Ignoring his gesture, she began haughtily, ". . . and I
refuse to accept your resignation."

"I am sorry, Ma'am. Deeply sorry, but we must consider the King and not further aggravate his position."

Agitatedly she walked backwards and forwards across
the room, finally pausing by a window, staring out over
the gardens. Then, without turning, "Oh how I detest that
Earl Grey . . . and his stupid Vig government." She came
back to face Richard, smiling, the outburst over. "I'm

sorry, Richard. Can you forgive such childish tantrums, for of course ve must both support the King."

He took her hand, raising it to his lips. "Happen what may, Ma'am, I am still your devoted servant and admirer . . ."

"You vill not leave the court? You vill remain my friend and adviser . . . vithout office?"

"As long as I can be of service to you, Ma'am, I will remain at Court."

"Then I myself vill take the personal satisfaction of informing the Prime Minister that having accepted your resignation . . . the post of Queen's Chamberlain shall remain vacant."

Despite the enthusiasm displayed at the coronation, the mood of the people soon slipped back to its old anger, with an even greater violence, and looking for a whipping-boy, became fanatically prejudiced against Adelaide. It was she who was influencing the King. Billy wasn't against reform; only that damned, sandy-haired frau.

New government after new government was formed; prime minister after prime minister voluntarily resigning, or being forced to resign. It was becoming more obvious that unless the Reform Bill did become law, the country would be plunged into revolution.

Perhaps it was the heat of that early June day that set all the Tory peers thinking of their country houses . . . the coolness of their spacious rooms . . . the fragrance of their gardens as compared with the stinking, fetid smell of London, for after a brief consultation they all agreed they would refrain from voting whatsoever, and so leave the road clear for the passing of the confounded bill.

London went mad with delight. Illuminations suddenly appeared on every building and house, and as part of the jollifications, the mobs went round breaking the windows of Tory Peers, and all others who failed to illuminate or put out bunting.

No one was more gratified than William that the nightmare was over, but Adelaide's fears were intensified, so deep was her conviction that in giving the people better wages and living conditions, they were giving them more power, and with this power in their hands, revolution could still come about.

William tried to set her mind at rest. "You're wrong, my love. 'Tis for the best. 'Twill take time for the reforms to come about . . . we shall hardly notice the process."

"But they hate me! Vy?"

"That will all fade away now. Try to understand. Be patient, my love."

"Patient? Ven have I not been patient? But I vill show them. Tonight, I am due to attend a concert in Hanover Square, and . . ."

"But Great God, Adelaide, listen to those crowds outside! You must not go! I forbid you! 'Twould be positively dangerous!"

". . . and I insist on going. Vat vould they say if I cancel the visit? Craven-hearted, German frau. More lampoons . . . more sarcasm in the news-sheets. You say their mood vill now have changed, so vat have I to fear?"

William made a gesture of hopelessness. "Because tonight . . . the excitement has gone to their heads . . . they're liable to go wild . . . berserk . . . do mad, crazy things . . ."

"I shall be safe in my carriage vith coachman and footmen . . ."

"I suppose I ought to accompany you . . . if you still insist on going . . . but I hate these damned musical evenings . . ."

"There's no need, Villiam, I assure you. Lady Brownlow is accompanying me. She, I am confident, has no fear."

"It is not a matter of fear, Adelaide, but of safety. Some gentleman must accompany you. Who better than Richard Howe?"

Adelaide bowed her head in acquiescence. "If you insist, Villiam. Lord Howe does, I believe, enjoy a concert. I vill include his vife in my party."

Lady Harriet, however, begged to be excused much to Adelaide's secret satisfaction. As they drove to Hanover Square, Richard by her side and Lady Brownlow opposite, conversation was stilted, each of them tense and alert for any sign of trouble. The mobs were out and about along the whole route, but beyond shouts, which in the closed carriage they could not distinguish, the journey was uneventful, as was their reception at the ball, the majority of the audience being composed of the nobility.

The rousing overture quickly dispelled her apathy and when more soothing cadences followed, she was gently transported to another world, forgetting all pestilential politics and its accompanying fears.

Once she glanced up at Richard, obviously enjoying the music, a faraway look in his eyes. As though aware of her scrutiny, he lowered his gaze so that their eyes met. For a brief second, they glimpsed each other's innermost feelings, then trembling, Adelaide turned her eyes back to the stage. She must be on her guard. She must not be the seducer, yet she wished the concert need never end; so that she could go on feeling Richard's nearness.

The crowd seemed to have grown, to have massed together, as though to greet them leaving the hall, but they allowed her and her attendants to get into their carriage without any trouble. It was when they reached Regent Street that another mob, recognizing the royal coach, became unruly, blocking the road and bringing the carriage to a standstill.

The footmen were quick to use their canes, but this only served to anger the rioters. One of them smashed in the carriage window, and then amid the cursing and jeering the vile insults could be heard.

"The Queen and her fancy-man! Where's poor old Billy-boy tonight? Left the old cuckold at home?"

Save for a quick in-drawn breath, Adelaide gave no sign, as in the same instant, Richard Howe thrust his body across hers, bidding Lady Brownlow to get behind him. Now with one arm around the Queen's shoulders, holding her so close to him that she could hear the pounding of his heart, he warded off first one evil face and then another that had the temerity to thrust itself through the broken window.

The coachman was flaying his whip at both mob and

horses, finally coaxing the frenzied animals into attempted movement, so that, unless they wanted to be trampled underfoot, the cursing ruffians had to step aside.

It was not until they were clear of the mob that Adelaide managed a whispered, "Thank you, Richard. Thank you."

Slowly he released his hold, taking her hand and kissing it. "It was nothing, Ma'am. Believe me, I would indeed give my life for you."

It was difficult with Lady Brownlow as an onlooker, for Adelaide knew that she had but to give Richard the lead, and the barrier would be down. He had kissed her hand many times . . . and many, many times she had wondered as to the beauty of a passionate lover's kiss. It was not for her. She was the Queen and she owed her loyalty to the King. Richard had a wife and several children. It was all so futile. Nothing could come of it . . . yet she would always cherish the moment when he had held her to his heart.

Outside *Clarence House*, the mob was surging backwards and forwards, repeatedly calling for the King. At first he had acceded to their demands, but as the night wore on, he became more anxious about the Queen, cursing himself and everyone around him, for allowing her to go out.

He gave an exclamation of relief as carriage wheels were heard. "Thank God. She's home," and heedless of servants and daughters sharing his vigil, dashed out to the coach to help her alight, the crowd peering gloatingly through the railings at this tidbit of royal domesticity. There were tears in his eyes as he kissed her. "I should never have let you go . . . or at least I should have accompanied you." He turned to Lord Howe. "In the name of Hell, what delayed you? I expected you . . ."

Before Richard could speak, Adelaide interrupted, "It was the mob, William. They held up the coach . . ."

"They held up the coach! The Queen's coach! God blast their eyeballs! Where were the troops?" William's voice was apoplectic. Then calming down, "But you, my love? Are you hurt? Were they very alarming?"

They had now reached the safety of the house. "No, Villiam, no . . . thanks to Richard. He vas vonderful . . . so brave . . ."

"It was the Queen, Sir, who was brave. Not a murmur of fear from either lady . . ."

"My Queen is always brave . . . My God, I need a drink after all that . . . and you . . . all of you . . ." and leading the way into the library, he himself poured the drinks.

"Now tell me everything that happened."

As Richard and Adelaide, between them, recounted the full story, William frequently punctuated it with curses and obscenities.

"Really, Villiam, there's no need for you to be so angry."

"Angry! Damn them! I'll show them just how angry I am! Tomorrow, I'm expected in the City, to be dined and wined by the Lord Mayor and Corporation. They'll wait . . . and go on waiting. I refuse to go. Where were the Mayor's preparations for the Queen's safety? Too scared to go out, I'll wager. Skulking within the Guildhall . . . the cowards! I'll teach them . . . I'll teach them."

"Villiam . . . do not be so hasty. Sleep on it. Do nothing to anger the people." She went up to him kissing him gently on the cheek. "And now I vould go to my room." She smiled at Lord Howe. "And again, Richard, my thanks."

He bent low, raising her hand to his lips and the pressure of his mouth, unnecessarily hard, was strangely disturbing. "I am your devoted servant, Ma'am."

Had he, or the King, or Lady Brownlow, waiting in the background, noticed her rising color?

Left alone, the two men faced each other, King and commoner. Then the King spoke.

"I, too, Richard, owe you much gratitude . . ."

"Nonsense, Sir. Any man would have done the same . . ."

"I do not only refer to tonight's incident . . ."

"Sir?"

"Your friendship with the Queen. I am glad of it. She is young. She needs young companionship. Life without you would be dull and tedious for I am too tired to accompany her, save on state occasions. Here at home, I am an old bore, only wanting to doze . . ."

For once, Richard was at a loss as to how to reply and could only stammer, "Sir, although I no longer hold office, I am proud that the Queen still desires my company."

William put a hand on the young man's shoulder. "Your office shall be restored, Richard. In the meantime, be assured of my everlasting thanks . . ."

Back in his own suite, Richard abruptly dismissed his valet. He wanted to be alone . . . to examine his disturbing thoughts and emotions. Obviously, the King was aware of his devotion to Adelaide and was prepared to turn a blind eye up to a certain point. What was it about the Queen that had captured his heart? She was not beautiful . . . not near so handsome a woman as his wife, but she had that dignity which Harriet so sorely lacked.

Did he want an affair with the Queen? With William's present attitude it would not be difficult. That Adelaide returned his affection, he was sure, but might it not be that she was lonely, longing for friendship, nothing more? At first he had pitied her, but now it was something much more intimate. Long into the night, he wrestled with his own feelings. He was a married man with a large family. Until now, he had always upheld dignity and honor. There was neither dignity nor honor in a clandestine love affair.

Yet he knew he would go on serving her . . . and loving her . . . to the end of time . . . Never, though, never would he force the issue, for to do so, would be to bring about her ruin . . . perhaps the ruination of the English monarchy.

It was some weeks later that Lady Brownlow broached the subject.

"Are you aware, Ma'am, that certain newspapers are making much of your friendship with Lord Howe?"

Intent on an intricate piece of embroidery, Adelaide spoke, without raising her head. "Of course. Both the King and I have seen the news-sheets."

"Then, Ma'am, would it not be wiser . . .?"

"Viser? In vat vay? *Truth vill always find its vay*. I am a loyal vife. Lord Howe is a loyal husband . . . and a loyal subject."

But when that night, as she lay in bed, listening to William's loud snores, the thought came as it did every night. How wonderful it must be to be loved and cherished by a man as young and handsome as Richard Howe, and that they were both free to give full expression to their passion.

9

The year 1833 started badly. After the winter season in Brighton, William and Adelaide returned to London to find a diversity of troubles awaiting them.

One of their first visitors was Frederick Fitzclarence, bursting with indignation that his post as Governor of the Tower of London had been made redundant.

"Well? What do you expect me to do about it?" bellowed his father.

"Sir . . . you are the King!"

"Yes . . . what of it?"

". . . Well, I am your son. Surely you can reverse the government's decision."

"To what end? The pay is but paltry . . ."

"I agree, but to be removed from one's post is so humiliating."

There was nothing he could do and the angry young man went away, hurling invectives at both the government and his father.

The invectives, however, were neither so violent nor so loud as those hurled at the Chapel of St. Paul, by William. Encouraged by Adelaide's kindly outlook on the late Mrs. Jordan, he had ordered a bust of the actress to be presented to the Chapel and had been filled with fury at its refusal.

"Why in God's name, could they accept one of Peg Woffington, and not of Dorothy Jordan?"

Adelaide tried to calm him. "Perhaps George vould like to have it . . . a bust of his mother . . . to pass down to his family."

Her tact worked, but she was becoming alarmed over William's increased irritability and violent outbursts of temper. She had now come to expect this behavior every spring, and did her utmost to shield him from bad news and awkward situations.

Christmas had been marred for them by the obvious worsening of Princess Louise Weimar's condition. To enable Adelaide to watch over her, they had brought her back to Windsor, but despite all the love and devotion, the sixteen-year-old princess died in March.

William was surprised at the intensity of his grief, so attached had he become to the invalid girl. Never were he and Adelaide so grateful that George Cambridge continued to live with them.

If only the Duchess of Kent could have been more cooperative, life would have been much easier for Adelaide.

"Why does she persist in refusing all our invitations?" William fumed. "Victoria should be coming to me to receive instructions about the monarchy . . ."

"Victoria is still very young . . ."

"Not too young to be trailed up and down the country by that old harridan of a mama. Not too young to meet mayors and be presented with loyal addresses . . ."

"Do not vex yourself, Villiam . . ."

"I am vexed. I know why she doesn't visit us. My

children . . . and my grandchildren, are not good enough. She thinks they will contaminate her darling Victoria."

It was the Duchess' visit to the Isle of Wight that sent him into his worst fury. Sailing in the cutter *The Emerald* which he had generously placed at her disposal, she was demanding naval salutes wherever they went. William instantly ordered that the salutes must cease, but the Duchess ignored him. There was nothing for it but to have the regulations altered. From then onward, the Royal Standard was only to be saluted when the King or Queen was on board.

The government had now offered to reinstate Lord Howe as Adelaide's chamberlain on condition that he would not oppose the government, but Richard refused this undertaking . . . with Adelaide's full support. She was quite content to do without a chamberlain but to appease William . . . and the government . . . she eventually appointed Lord Denbigh, only availing herself of his services on formal occasions, Richard Howe still remaining at Court . . . unpaid.

It was from the furtive whispering going on between her ladies and maids-in-waiting, that Adelaide guessed there was a tidbit of scandal being discussed, a little more titillating than usual. Eventually it transpired that one of her maids, Caddie, was *enceinte,* and rumor was rife that the King was responsible. Adelaide refused to discuss the ugly business, either with her ladies, the girl or William, but when Caddie requested that she should be excused her court duties in order to accompany her mother on a visit to the Continent, Adelaide turned unusually awkward.

"Ven you took service vith me, you agreed to the usual number of months."

"Yes, Ma'am, but . . ."

"I cannot release you. You remain here until you have completed your period of service."

The girl scowled and curtsied and made her exit. Caddie was one of her few failures. Her manners were not up to the required standard, thrusting herself into the conversations of her older ladies; reveling in gossip and retelling of bawdy stories. Perhaps William had talked nonsense with her . . . even to the extent of a naughty story . . . but nothing more. Of this Adelaide was sure. Caddie was the type to seek sympathy and a hearing by inventing stories even when they were against herself.

The passing months proved Adelaide's wisdom. Thank God she had had the sense and the trust not to approach William for there was no child. Yet she felt the lifting of a load, when Caddie made her departure, the laughing-stock of the Court.

Christmas had come round once again and the King and Queen with their vast family were as usual at Brighton. All the Fitzclarences were there; husbands and wives and a veritable army of children, Adelaide and William adoring each and every one of them.

For weeks now, Adelaide had been scouring the Brighton toy-shops, and boxes of toys and gifts were arriving daily from London. A huge fir-tree, the biggest obtainable, had been set up in the banqueting hall, and she herself had spent hours decorating it with gilded nuts, fruits and hundreds of candles.

Last night there had been a Christmas Eve dinner and assembly. Dear Mrs. Fitzherbert, now seventy-seven, had been one of the principal guests together with her adopted daughters, Minney and Maryanne and their husbands.

As usual, George Fitzclarence had eyes for no one but Minney Seymour. Poor George, but it had indeed been good to see William so happy in their company; to hear him and Maria laughing over old times despite all the heartache the old lady had suffered. Adelaide had been able to share the joke when Maria laughingly asked, "Have you, Sir, heard the latest rumor concerning you and me?"

William pretended to be shocked. "What have we been doing, dear lady?"

Maria was quick to retort. "There was a time, Sir, when I was very partial to you . . . in preference to George. No, Sir. I am referring to the story that I am endeavoring to woo you and the Queen over to the Catholic faith."

William nodded. "Yes. We have heard it. Ridiculous. Damned ridiculous. It's taken the Queen all these years to teach me to be a Christian . . . let alone any particular faith."

Adelaide was recalling last night's conversation as, resting in bed, she sipped her morning tea. It seemed that the people were still looking for any provocation to start more trouble. The promised reforms were so tardy in coming about, that after the first elation, impatience was taking its place.

William still rose early, taking about an hour and a half over his toilet and dressing. He might be an aging man, but when she thought of the vast, gross, dribbling hypochondriac that his brother had become, she felt an immense gratification and thankfulness.

There was a tap on the door and a child's voice piped, "May I come in, dear Queenie?"

"Come in, my little *liebchen,* come in."

Wilhelmina Kennedy-Erskine, born the day her grandfather succeeded to the throne, came slowly into the room. She paused as though considering her next move. Then having curtsied in a most creditable manner for a three-year-old, threw aside all restraint, rushed up, and climbed on to the bed, giving Adelaide a bear-like hug and kiss.

"It's Christmas Day, dear Queenie. When will the party be ready?"

"Four o'clock, *liebchen.*"

Mina sighed. "What a long, long time. I think I will now go and see the dear King."

Going over to the communicating door, she again tapped and listened.

It was Jemmet, the King's valet, who opened it.

"Come in, Miss Mina. You're just in time."

William, in his dressing-robe, with a towel round his shoulders, was sitting with head bent over a silver basin but nevertheless, Mina remembered her curtsey and then with hands behind her back, surveyed her grandfather.

"You've had your hair washed, Grandpapa?"

"All except the rinse . . . and seeing it's Christmas morning, how about you doing it?"

"May I? Oh, Grandpa! I would like that."

Jemmet had by now produced a low stool and lifting Mina, handed her an open bottle of rose-water.

"Now over my hair, Mina . . ."

"I'll be careful, Grandpapa . . ."

Slowly, the child tipped up the bottle and poured out its contents, filling the room with fragrance. When it had all gone, she stepped down, moved round to face the King to see the effects of her handiwork.

By now Jemmet was rubbing dry the grey curls and the King, opening his arms, took Mina on to his knee.

"And where is my Christmas Day kiss?" he demanded.

Mina willingly complied, sniffing appreciatively.

"You do smell sweet, Grandpapa. I wouldn't fuss over having my hair washed if I could have rose-water."

"When you grow up, my sweet, you can have everything you wish . . ."

"Everything? Then I shall have a party every day. Are you coming to the party this afternoon?"

"Of a certainty. I wouldn't dare miss dear Queenie's Christmas party."

Long before four o'clock, nannies from the various families were endeavoring to marshal their young charges into some semblance of order as they gathered in the long corridor leading into the Dragon Room. Where did they all come from? To begin with there were eight married Fitzclarences, each with two or three children; some more. There were nine young Howes, and it was Lord Howe now bidding each little boy to take a girl partner, and to form an orderly line.

Promptly at four o'clock, the double doors were opened and the King's band struck up a marching tune, which as the children marched into the room, was almost drowned by their long-drawn-out "oohs" and "ahs."

The Christmas tree was ablaze with myriads of candles guarded by lackeys, so that no child should run the risk of being burned. The huge dining table had been moved to the end of the room and scores of small white-painted tables had taken its place; each bearing two or three gaily wrapped parcels, and each table displaying a child's name.

The band ceased playing. The major-domo's loud voice called for silence. Then William and Adelaide entered, and the small guests, following their well-rehearsed instructions, curtsied and bowed. On behalf of the Queen, it was William who welcomed the guests and wished them a Happy Christmas, and then, hilarious as a schoolboy himself shouted:

"Now come and find your gifts."

What a mad scramble! Those who could read were weaving in and out among the tables; while mamas and papas were helping the toddlers. Then what delight, as wrapping papers were torn off every kind of toy imaginable. Adelaide was having difficulty in restraining her tears; always on these occasions she remembered her beloved little Elizabeth. She should have been here . . the future Queen of England.

As usual, the Duchess of Kent had refused the invitation, and although Adelaide had a sincere affection for Princess Victoria, she wryly told herself that the prim, well-brought-up little girl, would have indeed been out of her depth with this vociferous, carefree crowd of children

10

As Adelaide slowly paced the deck of the *Royal George,* her spirits rose at the thought of being back home once again. It had been wonderful revisiting all the familiar places of her childhood, meeting her relatives, being entertained; noting their envy of her rich clothes and jewels; their surprised acceptance at the expensive gifts she had taken for one and all; and their amazement at the loyal court who accompanied her . . . but now . . . home meant England . . . with William.

This visit had never been her idea, but after that last exhausting season in Brighton, dinners and assemblies almost every night, William had made all the necessary arrangements without consulting her.

She had protested. Although she did indeed feel the need of a rest, she feared to leave William, especially in the spring . . . the time when he was most liable to his brain-storms. She had argued that she would rather wait until her brother could come for her. William countered, that surely with Richard Howe and Lord Denbigh in charge, nothing could go wrong. Like any other loving wife, she protested that she hated leaving him, but again he pointed out that with two married daughters living with him at Windsor, he would be well looked after.

Now she had been away for six weeks. She did indeed feel much better for the rest. She had treatment from a German doctor and her cough was much relieved. How would she find William?

She looked up at Lord Howe, walking beside her.

"Are you not pleased, Richard, to see that English shore again?"

"Indeed, Ma'am, yes, but speaking for myself and Lady Howe, we have indeed enjoyed visiting the German courts."

"I am glad that Lady Harriet has enjoyed it. She is so gay and lively. I feel deeply in her debt, that she spares you so much to attend me at Vindsor."

To silence the gossips, she had insisted that Lady Howe accompany them, taking with her other young people, including William's daughter Elizabeth and her husband, Lord Errol. With Lady Brownlow as her lady-in-waiting they had formed an amicable party. Yet even so, there had been sarcastic rantings in the news-sheets, complaining of the eleven carriages that had gone over with them, together with the necessary large number of coachmen, footmen, ladies' maids and valets; comparing the retinue with that which had accompanied her on her arrival as a bride.

"I vonder how ve shall find the King?" She found herself speaking her thoughts aloud.

"All the reports have been good, Ma'am."

"I know, but Villiam can be . . . how do you say . . . not truthful, to ease my mind . . ."

"Lady Sydney or Lady Erskine would have informed us, Ma'am . . ."

"I know . . . but . . . all the same, I am so glad we are home."

William, waiting her arrival at *Clarence House*, was all impatience. For hours now, much to his gratification, the crowds had been gathering in the gay, bunting-dressed streets. Surely that was proof that the mass of people loved their queen! When the cheers became audible, growing from a whisper to a veritable barrage of applause and clapping, he knew his wife was home again. Out of the front door and down the steps he dashed and the moment she was out of the carriage she was in his arms. Then in his excitement, not only was he kissing his daughter, but also Lady Brownlow, much to everyone's merriment; but for William, their mirth meant only one thing; the last dreadful six weeks of loneliness were over.

Adelaide searched her husband's tell-tale face. Dear God, how tired he looked; how ill. No, he was perfectly well, he protested, but willingly admitted his joy that she was home.

Then all the children came running, gathered together to welcome home their "dear Queenie," and as Adelaide kissed each one, she realized why England was now home. She belonged to William and these children. They held her love and her heart.

They had barely settled down in Brighton for the winter season when the trouble started again. It was William's own fault. During her absence, Lord Melbourne's cabinet had succeeded Lord Grey's. Now for no clear reason William had dismissed Melbourne. The trouble-makers immediately accused Adelaide as the cause of the King's action, the news-sheets subjecting her to more abuse than ever, placards blatantly displaying, *"The Queen has done it all."* Adelaide thanked God they were in Brighton, for she felt that to have been in London would have meant real danger. She still believed in the possibility of a revolution. If only William had dismissed Melbourne before her return, then she would not have been the whipping-boy.

The most ignominious part of the whole business was that George Fitzclarence and his sister Elizabeth and her husband, Lord Errol, were three of her chief accusers.

Christmas had come and gone again. The same children's parties; the same assemblies and balls. Once the New Year was in, Adelaide tried to slow down their entertaining, for both she and William were feeling the strain.

William was still an early riser; a moderate eater and drinker, for he was determined to safeguard his health. He ordered his day on a strict routine; breakfasting with the Queen and any of his family who cared to join them at half past nine, having only a cup of coffee and two pieces of toast. *The Times* and *Morning Post* would next be dealt with, commenting aloud on their most provocative articles. Then to work on state papers until lunch-time . . . a meal of two lamb chops and two glasses of sherry. During the afternoon he would sleep or on rare occasions, to humor Adelaide, he would accompany her on a visit or a drive. Another sleep until dinner-time—another simple meal and then bed at eleven o'clock.

The thin, pale January sun was attempting to break through, when, having finished breakfast, Adelaide excused herself. It was just as well, for almost simultaneously William caught sight of a snippet of news, informing the world in general that the Queen, at long last was to present him with an heir.

At first William felt only sardonic amusement, muttering to himself, "What damn stuff is this?" of which the hovering footman took but little notice, being accustomed to the King's outspoken comments. When, however, shortly afterwards, his daughter, Augusta, sought an audience with him, his amusement turned to anger.

"Do you mean to say you've known of this rumor for some time?"

"Why yes . . . Papa . . . we all know . . ."

"All? All? And who are all?"

"My brothers and sisters . . . the ladies and gentlemen of the Court . . . even the servants . . ."

William's anger had now reached a new peak of fury.

"Do you listen to servants' gossip? To what the Court is saying . . . yet you keep me in the dark. . ."

"Why, Papa . . . we thought . . . naturally . . . that the Queen would have informed you . . ."

"Then why so anxious to tell me this morning . . . ?"

"Because . . . because . . . the papers . . ."

"Bah! The papers! They pay the servants for any tidbit of gossip . . . real or imaginary. I am ashamed that you . . . my daughter should believe . . ."

"As I said before, Papa . . . 'tis not I alone. Why, George only yesterday told me . . ."

"Go on . . ."

"That the Queen is now between two or three months gone . . ."

"Enough! I will see George." His voice suddenly quietened. "But suppose this was true? Why the interest? Why the hint of scandal?"

Augusta floundered. "Well, I suppose . . . because of the Queen's age . . . her delicate health. Then there are those who wonder why Lord Howe does not now attend Her Majesty so much . . ."

"Silence, girl! How dare you! Are you suggesting . . . or even listening to suggestions that . . ." He shook his head in bewilderment. "How you can forget for one moment the immensity of the Queen's goodness towards you and your children, passes my understanding. I suppose you heard that other edifying morsel of gossip concerning Caddie and me?"

"Yes, Papa . . ."

"But you did not come running to admonish me . . . nor to the Queen with your sympathy?"

"No, Papa . . ."

"No, because you did not wish to quarrel with me. To fall out of favor with the Queen seems less important, so you join in with the gossips. The Queen knew all about the Caddie business, but not one word . . . not one question did she ask, just dealing with the girl in her own quiet way, knowing it to be utter rubbish. She trusted me . . . just as I trust her. From now on, you will do all in your power to silence this fiendish, mischievous gossip."

Augusta was weeping copiously, but William was far from feeling sorry for her . . . "and if you cannot find anything more profitable to do at Windsor than indulge in such filth, you can go elsewhere to live."

By the time he met Adelaide he had cooled down and was able to smile with her, as they spoke of the matter. "How I vish it vas true, Villiam," she said, lifting his hand to her cheek . . . "but ve have each other."

The health of each was indeed a concern to the other. William's asthma was worsening, as was Adelaide's cough, but their engagements continued to make their demands. Sometimes Adelaide had to go without William; at other times it was Adelaide who was too ill to put in an appearance.

*   *   *

Never had Adelaide felt parting with a loved one so keenly as when George, Prince of Cambridge, returned home to Hanover for military training. Bringing him up, as though he was her own son, had helped to heal the wound left by the death of her baby. True, there were the grandchildren but George would always be her dearest.

William, too, felt the pangs of his departure and having watched the carriage out of sight, put his arm around Adelaide as they went indoors.

" 'Twill not be long before he's back . . . and we know why . . ." He squeezed her arm affectionately.

"I am not so sure, Villiam. George is a strange boy. He thinks for himself. He vill not be dictated to."

"You mean about marrying Victoria? Bah . . . he's but sixteen years old . . . When a boy's that age, he's full of idealistic, romantic notions . . ."

"But George is so emphatic . . . not particularly about Vicky . . . but about marriage in general . . ."

"He'll soon change some of his notions now that he's in the army. When he realizes the full impact of marrying his cousin . . . being consort to the Queen of England . . . he'll fall in with our plans."

"I vish I thought so, Villiam. Nothing vould make me more happy than to see them married . . . but . . ."

Adelaide's doubts were soon heightened when the Duchess of Kent invited two of her nephews from the Coburg family to visit her at Kensington.

William was furious.

"She's planning to marry Vicky to one of them," he stormed, "and without consulting me . . . It's that damned brother of hers . . . Leopold . . . always interfering . . . always pushing the Coburgs. I loathe the family."

"But ve must entertain them, Villiam . . ."

"What? Entertain them when they've come here to oust George from being the consort? I will not tolerate them."

"But, Villiam . . . Vicky is only sixteen . . . surely the Duchess vill not vant her to marry as yet . . ."

"There's no telling what that woman wants. I'll scotch her plans. I'll invite other princes to come to court. I'll

orbid the Duke of Saxe-Coburg and his precious sons to
set foot in England."

"Villiam. Villiam. You cannot do these things. And
who do you suggest inviting?"

"Oh . . . oh . . . the young Duke of Brunswick and the
Prince of Orange and his son . . ."

"But vat about George?" the Queen asked anxiously.

William had no answer, but under Adelaide's soothing
nfluence, his anger subsided, and the Coburg brothers
vere entertained most royally, leaving the country without any definite settlement of a proposal of marriage,
much to William and Adelaide's great relief.

Adelaide handed the note across to William. As he
read, a scowl suffused his face, and a torrent of obscene
abuse escaped him.

"Villiam. Villiam. If the Duchess does not vish to dine
vith us on my birthday . . . it is not an occasion for such
orrible language . . ."

"But it is. It is an insult to refuse . . ."

"Then she prefers to honor you for she says she vill
ine here at Vindsor on your birthday next veek and vill
ring Victoria . . ."

"If she thinks that she can humor me . . . she is making
big mistake. She has gone too far. I will not have you
umiliated."

All week, William ruminated on the Duchess' casual
ehavior; and being in London decided to call on her at
Kensington. To his surprise she had already left for Wind-
or, but to his far greater surprise he discovered that she
ad annexed another seventeen rooms to her apartments;
ooms that she had asked for twelve months ago; rooms
hat he had refused her.

All the way to Windsor, his anger rose to a new pitch.
The woman must be stopped. She was over-riding him. By
God, he would let her know he was King.

He barely spoke to Adelaide, who, knowing him in all
is moods, realized something had upset him, allowing
im to go to his dressing-room and Jemmet's ministra-
ons, without pressing for an explanation.

There were a hundred guests at the dinner. The Duchess of Kent, her rose-satin gown billowing out like a full-blown peony, was seated on one side of William, while on the other, his ageing spinster sister, Augusta, beamed gleefully. Dressing-up and eating were the only pastimes now left to her. Opposite them, seventeen-year-old Victoria, short and plump like her mother, primly scanned the guests, her demureness hiding the inner excitement of dining with the Court at Windsor.

The fact that William blatantly ignored the Duchess seemed to go unnoticed and the meal passed off uneventfully, everyone too busy enjoying the rich, delicious food.

Then the Queen rose, smiling and looking down at her husband, proposing that they should drink to the health and long life of the King. The response was loud and loyal.

William slowly stumbled to his feet.

"I trust in God that my life may be spared for nine months longer, after which period, in the event of my death, no regency would take place. I should then have the satisfaction of leaving the royal authority to the personal exercise of that young lady . . ." He paused, to point dramatically at Victoria, *". . . and not in the hands of a person near me . . ."* He gave a contemptuous glance at the uncomfortable, flush-faced Duchess, *". . . who is herself incompetent to act with propriety in the station in which she would be placed. I have no hesitation in saying that I have been insulted . . . grossly and continually insulted . . . by that person, but I am determined to endure it no longer, a course of behavior so disrespectful to me."* He was now shouting, loud and excited, *"I would have her know that I am the King, and I am determined to make my authority respected."*

William sat down. No one spoke. Then Victoria burst into tears, as did Adelaide, trying to restrain the Duchess from leaving the table.

Beside herself with mortification, the Duchess was demanding that Victoria should accompany her, giving orders that her carriage should be called immediately, for they were returning to Kensington there and then.

Adelaide tearfully accompanied them to their apartments and finally succeeded in persuading her sister-in-law to remain the night, by repeated assurances that William would apologize.

William, however, determinedly refused.

"Why should I? Since the day she met us in my mother's drawing-room on the occasion of our marriage, she has sought to insult me and humiliate you. There shall be no more of it. I have decided that Sophia and her family shall live at Kensington—with Sophia holding the rank of Royal Housekeeper. The Duchess of Kent shall have a mistress . . . and a Fitzclarence at that!"

Within a week or two, William's good humor was restored, with the remarriage of his daughter Augusta to Lord John Gordon. The wedding was a brilliant affair, held in the Royal Chapel at Windsor, her father having completely forgiven her for listening to the gossip about the Queen. He could never be angry for long with any of his children.

Yet the gossip was to become rife again, for in October, Lady Howe, only thirty-seven, died five weeks after the birth of her tenth child.

Adelaide was all compassion, taking the new baby and younger children into her care, and appointing Richard's eldest daughter, Lady Georgina Curzon as a maid of honor. The gossips smirked at each other. A crafty move to have the children at Windsor. What more natural than that their father should spend still more time at the Castle?

Not within living memory could the townsfolk of Brighton remember such snowstorms. Drifts, ten feet high, ranged themselves along the Pavilion walls and turned the Steyne into a huge, fairy-tale playground, assuring that the Christmas of 1836 would be a Christmas to be remembered for its skating and sleighing parties.

As usual, the Pavilion was the center of the festivities, Adelaide again giving her parties for the children in addition to her other vast entertaining. All the big, newly built houses had been rented by the aristocratic hangers-on who followed the Court to and fro from London to Brighton, vying one with the other as to who could entertain on the most lavish scale.

This year, Maria Fitzherbert was content to remain in the background, instead of being Adelaide's chief adviser. Now turned eighty, she was beginning to feel her age, but her two adopted daughters, Minney and Maryanne, together with their families were always at the royal table. Indeed, since William had become King, he had insisted on treating Maria and her family as if they were royal, and was delighted that Maria and his elderly sister Augusta had become close friends.

Deep down, Adelaide did not like Brighton, but never complained to William, knowing his enjoyment both of the proximity of the sea and the frolics of the gaudy, ostentatious Pavilion. The end of February, however, came round and for her at least it was a joy to return to Windsor.

11

Adelaide scarce knew how to break the news to William. A messenger had just brought word of the death of Maria Fitzherbert.

Bracing herself, she went into the library where the King was busy with the morning mail. He looked up in surprise for she rarely interrupted him until lunch-time.

"I . . . I . . . have just received . . ."

"Some bad news, Adelaide. I can tell by your face . . . what is it?"

"Our dear friend, Mrs. Fitzherbert . . ."

"Dead? Maria dead?" His voice was but a whisper. "God rest her soul."

"She died peacefully . . . yesterday . . ."

"Easter Monday? She would like that . . . she was deeply religious . . . Poor Maria . . . she had much to contend with. You know . . . she still loved my brother . . . and he loved her . . ."

"Despite all the mistresses of vich I have heard so much?"

"Despite them all. I shall miss her. It is as though part of my life has ended . . . a time when we were all so young and foolish." He gave a big sigh. "My son George must represent me at the funeral. He too was fond of his Aunt Fitzherbert . . ."

"Yet she did not encourage him as a son-in-law?"

"No . . . one Guelph in the family was enough she said."

"Poor George. He has often told me of his love for Minney. He still loves her, you know. No vonder he and his vife, Mary, are alvays quarreling."

No sooner had Maria been laid to rest in the churchyard of St. John the Baptist, than news came that Adelaide's mother was seriously ill and unlikely to recover.

Adelaide was distraught. She longed to go to her mother, yet hated to leave William.

"Oh, Villiam, vat must I do?"

Ill, dejected and dispirited as he felt, he was quick to reply. "Do? Why, you must go to her immediately. Take Howe and Denbigh with you . . ."

"But I do not vish to leave you . . . I said never again vould ve bo parted . . ."

"This will be the last time, dear Queenie. I owe it to your mother . . . in that she gave you to me . . . Travel incognito and so avoid all the damned presentations and addresses . . ."

She was quickly on her way, her step-daughters assuring her that once again they would take great care of dear Papa.

She was only just in time, and when the last sad farewell had been said, she hurriedly took leave of her sister, Ida, Duchess of Weimar, and sped back to England. Uppermost in her mind was how she would find William, distressed first by the death of Maria, and now by the death of his mother-in-law for whom he had developed a sincere affection.

In order that the public should not be aware of her arrival at Tilbury, it was one of Lord Howe's carriages that awaited them, and Adelaide, herself feeling ill, thought longingly of the comfort of her own rooms. Soon she would be home.

She would liked to have enquired of the coachman or footmen, as to His Majesty's health, but her dignity forbade the familiarity.

Arriving at *Clarence House*, she knew a moment of fear when William was not on the steps . . . nor even in the hall to greet her.

"The King?" she demanded sharply of a nearby lackey.

"He is waiting in the library, Ma'am . . ."

She almost ran into the room, as the flunkeys opened the double doors. Although the day was warm with April sunshine, William was sitting over a huge fire; a rug around his shoulders; sitting crouched . . . huddled up . . . looking older than she had ever seen him.

She was down on her knees beside him, kissing him on both cheeks . . . waiting for his loving response, and when none came, she urged, "Villiam. I am home. Look at me. Are you ill?"

Slowly he raised his eyes, and it was then she saw the sorrow and grief. "Vat is it, Villiam? Vat has happened?" Her guttural speech was hoarse with anxiety.

"Sophia . . . Sophia . . ." and then the torrent of pent-up sobs was released, interspersed with, "My darling little Sophia . . . my eldest daughter . . . my beautiful little Sophia."

Adelaide gripped him by the arms. "No, Villiam, no! Not Sophia. She vas so healthy . . . how could it happen?"

He shook his head mournfully. "Why do women die in childbirth? God only knows . . . but why?"

She cradled him as she would have done a child. "It is God's vill, Villiam. Ve can but give thanks for the joy her years of loveliness have given you."

Gradually, his sobs lessened. Her comforting arms and voice seemed to renew his strength, so that he was able to ask, "And you, dear Adelaide? I am a selfish monster that I think only of my own sorrows. How are you, dear heart?"

"Tired, dear Villiam, tired, but one night in my own bed and I shall be rested."

Next morning, however, found her so ill that the doctor gave strict orders that she must remain in bed for at least a week. She was distracted as to how William would take the news, and the doctor, knowing of her anxiety, agreed to tell the King that she was suffering from nothing more than physical exhaustion due to the family bereavement and the traveling involved.

Thankful to have her home again, William readily accepted the diagnosis, and when she protested that she must be up in time for her drawing-room the following week, he put his foot down, saying he would ask his sister Augusta to take her place.

Adelaide was only too happy to accept the suggestion. Her cough was much worse, and she did indeed feel the need of a rest, but there was the ever-present nagging fear of how William might behave . . . or what he might say, if she wasn't there to restrain him.

Augusta promised to be on her guard . . . but Augusta was old and deaf.

It was Lady Brownlow who, the day after the drawing-room, brought her the ill news . . . news that Adelaide insisted on hearing.

The Duchess of Kent and Princess Victoria were among the guests, attended by the Duchess' secretary, Sir John Conroy. It was common gossip as to the state of affairs existing between the Duchess and her secretary, but Adelaide had refused to believe, recalling how the Court had maligned her and Lord Howe.

Not so, however, with William, who, when he came face to face with the Duchess, cut her dead. Then he saw Sir John, and, wheeling round, shouted:

"Where is the Queen's Chamberlain? Denbigh, where the Hell are you?"

Lord Denbigh was at his side almost immediately. "That man," came the King's loud voice, as he pointed to Sir John. "What is that man doing in my throne room?"

A sudden hush came over the vast drawing-room. The last chattering voice was suddenly stilled.

"My Lord Chamberlain . . . turn that man out!"

There was nothing that Lord Denbigh could do but to approach Sir John with a few courteous words, and accompany him from the room.

With his departure, the chatter broke loose once again . . . only louder, more excited, but William was happy. He had scored once again over the Duchess of Kent, but Adelaide in her weakness felt only more depressed that there should be this antagonism; antagonism which again the young Princess Victoria had been forced to witness.

There was no doubt about it, William was failing but he resolutely refused to see a doctor, although Adelaide had by now insisted on the physician-royal living in . . . but carefully keeping out of the King's sight.

He had collapsed on several occasions; sometimes he was unable to walk upstairs unaided; and to Adelaide's great regret, they were both too ill to attend the ball given by William in honor of Princess Victoria's eighteenth birthday, and again it was old Aunt Augusta, who had to do the honors.

William had planned a *coup de grâce* against the Duchess in offering Victoria, as one of the coming-of-age presents, an establishment of her own. Victoria had been delighted; her mother furious; but later elated on hearing that neither William nor Adelaide would be at the ball.

By now, William had capitulated and had allowed the doctor to visit him, but stubbornly refused to go to bed, being wheeled around in a chair. He still held his councils each morning; and insisted the large house party for Ascot should go on as usual, and on June 4th the Castle was almost bursting with hundreds of guests and their servants.

Adelaide could stand the strain no longer and issued the order that the party should be dispersed so that she could take the King to Brighton, where he insisted he would make a quick recovery.

He was, however, too ill to be moved, and now thoroughly alarmed, Adelaide suggested that he should see the Archbishop of Canterbury.

William scoffed. "If you want to say some prayers for me, where's that son of mine, Augustus? Or George Cambridge's old tutor, Mr. Wood? Didn't you make him your chaplain? Let him do something to earn his corn!"

So Augustus Fitzclarence and Mr. Wood came and read morning prayer. To his own surprise, the King felt much comforted and insisted that his newly married daughter, Augusta, still living in the Castle, should read it to him every day.

Adelaide rarely left William's side. When he refused to go to bed, she lay on a day-bed by his side. Day after day, night after night, without undressing, she remained with him.

He was adamant in that he would have no bulletins issued, saying that he would not have his people alarmed, yet when on June 18th he remarked that he would like to live long enough to celebrate the anniversary of Waterloo, it was obvious that he knew the end was near.

By now, all his children were gathered at Windsor, and it was George Fitzclarence who saw to fulfilling his father's wish, bringing the flag that hitherto Wellington had brought each anniversary of Waterloo.

Stroking it lovingly, and then holding it to him, William smiled at those around him. *"Ah, that was a glorious day for England."*

He turned to George. "Thank you, my son." He hesitated. "Over the last few years . . . there have been times when we have not seen eye-to-eye . . . but then that happens in all families." His voice trailed away, and there was a far-away look in his eyes. "We were a happy family, were we not? Very happy." Then he looked George full in the face, taking his hand. "I have been a most fortunate man, my son, in having the love of two good women . . . you . . . you understand . . . and . . . and . . . should the Queen need help . . . you will . . ."

"Not only I, Father, but all of us. You know our love for her."

When he and Adelaide were alone again, William took a leather case from his pocket, and with a shaking hand gave it to the Queen. "For you, dearest and sweetest of women."

Wonderingly, Adelaide opened it, exclaiming in surprise at the magnificence of the diamond bracelet.

"But, Villiam . . . this is beautiful . . . but vy?"

"When I married you, I had no money to buy you diamonds. Do you remember you used your own jewels for your coronation crown?"

"I did not mind . . . it vas for us . . ."

"I wish I could have bought you more . . . you are worthy of so much more . . ."

She fastened the bracelet on her wrist and held it up so that the June sunlight caught the brilliance of the gems, splitting them into myriads of sparkling lights.

She kissed him gently. "Thank you so much, Villiam." Her voice was almost a whisper, and he felt the tears on her cheeks.

"Come, come, dear Queenie. Bear up . . . bear up. I feel so much better today."

He was indeed well enough to remember a man lying under sentence of death and to grant him a free pardon. He was well enough to send a message to Princess Victoria and well enough to refrain from inviting her to visit him, knowing that her mother would insist on accompanying her . . . and he had no wish to see the Duchess.

The Rev. Augustus Fitzclarence was now in constant attendance on his father, who now, quiet and uncomplain-

ng, found great comfort in prayer, as he lay, holding
Adelaide's hand, his head resting on her shoulder.

The day had been long and hot; the dusk and darkness
o slow in coming; now slow in going. Throughout the
night all the children had kept vigil with their step-
mother; sometimes wakeful; sometimes dozing, but Adelaide, with one arm around him, his head on her shoul-
er, never flinched in her uncomfortable position.

William's voice came low and unintelligible, save to
Adelaide, who murmured in reply, "I am here, William. I
ill not leave you." Unnoticed by their now semi-
onscious king, the Archbishop of Canterbury and Lord
Conyngham had joined the family.

They had not long to wait. With the coming of the
awn, a last long-drawn-out sigh told Adelaide she was a
widow.

As the doctor stepped forward to compose the body, so
Adelaide slipped to her knees by his side, as his sons and
daughters, comforting each other filed out with a silently
said goodbye to the father who had so loved them all . . .
despite cruel attacks of the press.

When the last one had gone, Adelaide rose, still dry-
eyed and composed, and stood for a moment regarding
the man with whom she had shared the throne of England
and a kind of love, born of duty and compassion. Gently,
he kissed him on the brow, and went out to join the
others.

12

She was wealthy. She was free . . . free to travel where
she wished . . . free to spend her money as she chose . .
free to live where her fancy took her.

After William had been laid to rest with his ancestors
at Windsor, she had lost no time in vacating the Castle
and returning to *Bushey*. Ida, and three of her children
had come to spend the summer with her and in the
peacefulness of the countryside, her sorrow and grief
gradually eased.

Victoria had been most considerate, allowing her to
take as many horses as she wished from the Windsor
stables together with any furniture or fittings from the
apartments. Yet all she had appropriated had been a
portrait of William and his family . . . with a painting of
Dorothy Jordan on the wall behind . . . and the silver cup
the King had used during his last illness.

Dear little Vicky. She had been so magnanimous about
William's children. At first, she had feared for their fu
ture, knowing of the Duchess of Kent's abhorrence of
them all, an abhorrence that she had instilled into her
daughter.

Once settled in at *Bushey,* she sent for George
Fitzclarence.

They greeted each other warmly . . . but wordlessly . .
the first time since the funeral. She joined him at the
window, where he stood staring out, lost in thought.

"The gardens, Sir, are very beautiful, are they not?"

"Indeed, Ma'am, their beauty makes my heart ache
Our garden at Brighton is but small . . ."

"Ah . . . did you go through vith the purchase of the
house in Brunsvick Square?"

"I did, Ma'am . . . and now I am dismayed at the prospect of how I shall pay off the mortgage . . ."

"Poor George . . . but it vas to talk of financial affairs that I asked you to call on me. Now there are no grace or favor apartments in any of the royal residences, I know that matters must be difficult for you all. I have already written the Queen."

" 'Twill be useless, Ma'am. She has no liking for us. I was compelled to ask for an audience to hand over the Windsor keys, which I hoped she would allow me to retain . . . but no such fortune. Adolphus has lost his lordship of Bedchamber, although he does keep command of the royal yacht. Frederick . . ."

"I know, George . . . I know . . . but I am pressing that Her Majesty continue all your allowances . . . as ven your father vas alive. After all, you are semi-royal . . . children of a King. In the meantime, you each have a legacy of £2,000, have you not, and equal shares in a £40,000 life insurance?"

"Yes, Ma'am, and we are indeed grateful for your concern . . ."

"There is something else." She had gone over to a bureau, taking out several bundles of letters, all neatly, securely tied.

"These are letters that passed between your parents . . . mostly letters written by your mother."

George's face was a picture of incredulous amazement. "Why, why . . . dear, dear, Queenie . . . such generosity . . I . . . we never expected . . ."

"Did you think I vould destroy them?"

"The Duchess of Kent burned those written by Madame Julie to the Duke . . ."

"Ah, yes, and vell I can remember your father's anger . . ."

"Speaking of Madame Julie, Ma'am, did my father ever inform you of her marriage since she returned to Canada?"

"Yes. She is now Princess Prospero Colonna. Her husband is a French nobleman, and now the dear lady enjoys a much wider social life than she ever did in England."

"Then I do indeed rejoice for her."

George Fitzclarence slowly shook his head. "You know, dear Queenie, you are the kindest, most generous-natured lady it has been my fortune to meet. These letters," he indicated the bundles, some still in his hands, ". . . my brothers and sisters . . . and our children will treasure them, and your loving concern will always be remembered." He cleared his throat to cover the emotion that was rising in his voice. "I did hear, Ma'am, that after Aunt Fitzherbert's death, letters written to her by the Duke of Kent, just friendly letters, had been returned to the Queen. I scarce dare think they are still in existence."

"Not if they fell into the hands of the Duchess. She has such fear that Mrs. Fitzherbert might have had a child . . . who could dispute Victoria's throne."

"Indeed yes. I had it on authority, that within a few days of her death, Wellington was going through her private papers, burning many of them there and then in the house. I did not tell Papa, knowing how vastly it would have disturbed him."

"Thank you for your consideration, George. It vould indeed have angered him . . . but tread varily, Sir, if you hope to continue your allowances from the Privy Purse."

She and Princess Augusta had gone to St. Leonard's for the winter. Despite the fact that Augusta was now seventy, she enjoyed the old lady's company. The only disappointment about the resort was that it did not come up to the doctor's expectations, for when she returned to London in March, her cough was as bad as ever.

Marlborough House had been designated to her as a town residence but although three hundred men had been working in it for six months, it was still far from habitable. There was nothing for it but to reside temporarily in her old home, *Clarence House,* bringing back memories of reform strife and William in difficult moods.

There was, however, the good news from the Queen

:hat she intended to continue the Fitzclarence allowances.

As dowager queen, protocol prevented her from attending the coronation, but when, on the great day, she heard the pealing of the bells, her heart went out to the young girl, remembering the many heartaches and anxieties that beset a queen. Sitting down at her desk, while the bells stirred up nostalgic disturbing memories, she wrote:

> *My Dearest Niece,*
>
> *The guns are just announcing your approach to the Abbey and as I am not near you and cannot take part in the sacred ceremony of your coronation, I must address you in writing to assure you that my thoughts and my whole heart are with you and my prayers are offered up to Heaven for your happiness and the prosperity and glory of your reign.*
>
> *Your most affectionate Aunt and Subject,*
>
> *Adelaide.*

Then the doctors had ordered her away to Malta, but not before the Duke and Duchess of Cambridge came home to England.

The Duke of Cumberland had now succeeded to the throne of Hanover, no woman being allowed to occupy it. Thus the Duke of Cambridge was no longer required as Regent, and perforce, had to return to England. While sympathizing with her brother-in-law, Adelaide at the same time was elated. It would be wonderful to have them living at *Cambridge House* . . . to have a woman friend of her own age . . . to have the company of her two pretty nieces . . . and George.

Dear, dear George. He had been like a son to her and William. Together they had watched over his education and upbringing, so that he should exemplify the perfect English gentleman . . . the ideal consort for Victoria.

Cruising in the Mediterranean, staying in white-walled villas of Malta and Gibraltar, were pleasant ways of escaping the cold and fog of the English winter, but all the time she yearned to be back. When the letter arrived from Victoria bursting with joy and excitement about her forthcoming marriage to her cousin Albert, Adelaide's heart sank with disappointment.

Why had George allowed Albert to supplant him? After all her hopes, and those of his parents? Deep down she knew the answer. He had such romantic ideas about marriage. No marriage of convenience for him.

Yet she was glad for Victoria, for both she and her mama had been living in a state of apprehension lest she should marry old Lord Melbourne, her Prime Minister. Victoria had not denied her liking for the fifty-eight-year-old gentleman. He was so gentle . . . so courteous . . . so attentive, and the delicious feeling that coursed through her whenever their hands met, was so exciting and thrilling.

Little wonder that the Duchess of Kent had come running to Adelaide for comfort and advice as she had done after the death of her husband, and later when she thought the raddled, debauched George IV had designs upon her daughter, Feodora.

Since William's death, she and Victoire had picked up the threads of their former friendship and all the evil, hurtful things had been forgiven . . . if not forgotten, the Duchess now bemoaning Victoria's cruel, hurtful, casual attitude towards her.

It was a splendid wedding. Apart from the fact that she still considered Albert had usurped what should have been George's position, she liked the bridegroom, especially when he showed a preference for her friendship against that of his mother-in-law. For the occasion, she wore a gown of cream velvet, trimmed with ermine, a rich setting for her magnificent pearls. Standing there she tried to remember how many weddings she had attended since she first came to England . . . how many brides she had kissed, wishing them happiness. When, the service over, Victoria left her husband's side to come and kiss her, the tears began to flow. Dear, dear Vicky.

That night she gave a family party at *Marlborough*

House. It was a great success. Everybody happy. All hatchets buried, until the health of the bridegroom was proposed. Then Augusta, Duchess of Cambridge, refused to stand. She was still feeling the indignity that her son was not the bridegroom.

Each spring, she returned to *Bushey*. It was as though the awakening countryside beckoned to her. She found a strange excitement in driving up the chestnut avenue, just bursting into leaf . . . strong, virile leaves pushing their way through protective, sticky buds like so many hands reaching out for the fresh, clean air and sunshine; then round by the rhododendron shrubbery, along by the herbaceous borders and the vast, expansive lawns, till the carriage came to a halt in front of the house.

There came the autumn of 1840 when she didn't go abroad. Princess Augusta was too ill to travel with her; too ill to be left, and when she died in September, it was Adelaide who remained with her to the end, holding her hand.

At Windsor, however, there was joy. Victoria was expecting her first child in November, and Adelaide was content to remain in London.

Marlborough House was now the scene of many a family assembly, alive with the comings and goings of the Fitzclarences and their children. She still held children's parties and took them to the circus and pantomimes. She might be a sick, ailing grandmother, but she had no intention of being a miserable one.

For the winter, she rented *Sudbury Hall* near Derby, but she was back in London by February for the christening of the Princess Royal, Victoria Adelaide, fondly named "Pussy" by her adoring parents . . . and again Adelaide was a godmother.

Back again to *Bushey*. Back again to *Sudbury*. Wherever she went, there was no improvement in her health. As Lord and Lady Brownlow's guest, she stayed at their country home at Belton. Lord Howe took her to stay with him and his family of ten children at Gopsall. Then back to *Sudbury*, where in a state of collapse she took to her bed. The doctors believed her to be dying and she, sensing their fear, demanded paper and pen, in order to write out the directions for her funeral.

> *I die in all humility . . . and I request my mortal remains be conveyed to the grave without any pomp or state . . . to be moved to St. George's Chapel, Windsor, where I request . . . as private and quiet a funeral as possible. I particularly desire not to be laid out in state, and the funeral to take place by daylight, no procession. The coffin to be carried by sailors. All those of my friends and relations who wish to attend may do so. My nephew, Prince Edward of Saxe-Weimar, Lord Howe and Denbigh . . . with my dressers and those of my ladies who wish to attend . . .*
>
> *I request not to be dissected nor embalmed . . .*
>
> *I shall die in peace with the world and full of gratitude for all the kindness that was ever shown to me and in full reliance to the mercy of our Savior Jesus Christ in whose hands I commit my soul.*
>
> *Adelaide R.*

She did not die, and as a thank-offering sent £3,000 to Malta Cathedral, and while the villagers of *Sudbury* gave thanks for the preservation of their beloved benefactress, the country went wild with joy at the birth of the Prince of Wales.

She was back at *Marlborough House* early in the New Year, but to avoid changes in temperature, her doctors ordered that she must keep to one room. Here she held her little court, friends and relations calling, bringing news of what was going on in the royal circle. She felt grieved that she was unable to attend the christening of the Prince of Wales, but a constant stream of visitors brought her all the minutest details of the occasion.

Her step-children and grandchildren were still constant visitors, looking up to Adelaide as a beloved mother.

George caused her most concern. His marriage was still proving most unhappy. Whether the fault lay with George or his wife, Adelaide could never decide.

Prior to his leaving for the trip to France, she teased him, "Now George . . . Paris in the springtime? I hope you are taking Mary."

"No, Ma'am. No. 'Tis a business trip." He was more than usually brusque and abrupt in his manner. She regarded him, a troubled frown on her face.

"The children? And Mary? Are they all well?"

"Perfectly, dear Queenie. And now I must bid you goodbye.'" He had bowed low and kissed her hand. There was something wrong. Of that she was sure. A strangeness that she had known in his father, indefinable, but positively there.

Monsieur L'Horlorge of the Rue de Rivoli gesticulated expansively, displaying his long, delicately tapered fingers.

"Oui. Mais certainement, Monsieur. I can make just the clock you want . . . to your own description . . . your choice of ornamentation . . ."

"These English aristocrats," he mused, "flaunting their wealth. Cannot he get his clock made in London?"

"You have been recommended to me as the best clock-maker in Paris." The Englishman had now taken a paper from his pocket, and placed it on the counter.

"This is as I wish the finished clock." Monsieur L'Horlorge stared at the paper. Instead of numerals for the hours, there were letters, M. D.A.W.S.O.N. D.A.M.E.R. He looked up at his customer. A gift for his mistress, without a doubt.

"Yes. That is how I desire it. Also this birthdate, engraved here. Now round the clock face I would have a coiled serpent to denote eternity. Would you, Monsieur, be so good as to make notes of my requirements. I wish to avoid any error."

The clock-maker wrote hurriedly, but paused to say hesitantly, "A clock to such a special design will be very costly . . ." His halting English was no better nor worse than his customer's French, but between them they managed to understand each other.

"That is no matter." The Englishman waved the suggestion aside. "Now above the serpent, surmounting the clock, I would have a basket containing forget-me-nots, while round the serpent, sprigs of rosemary . . . all in the best quality enamel . . ."

"It will take several months, Monsieur. I shall make it myself . . . it will be a labor of love . . ."

"How long? Eight months?"

"Non. Non, Monsieur. Cinque. Six . . ."

"I do not wish it to be delivered until the twenty-third of November. That gives you eight months. I want it to be perfection. State your price. Include your passage to London . . . and your stay at a hotel, for I wish you to deliver it in person . . . on this date . . . at this address."

Truly the Englishman was mad. He made a rapid calculation. Then doubled it and boldly stated his price.

The customer took out his notebook. "Here is a bill on Coutts' Bank. You can cash it before you begin work. Then I leave it to you. Please do not fail me."

Monsieur L'Horlorge bowed low as he opened the shop-door for his customer's exit, who about to step outside, turned and asked, "Could you direct me to St. Cloud? I would visit the cemetery there."

There was no doubt about it. This gentleman was truly odd, but to simplify directions, suggested that he should hire a carriage.

George Fitzclarence stared at the sunken, lurching headstone. He tried to read the inscription, already weather-worn and green with moss.

Dorothy Jordan

Poor, dear, darling Mama. Out here in a foreign country, alone save for Nannie Sketchley and the occasional visit from Frederick. He himself had been away in India.

His father had professed ignorance as to her loneliness, and reason for residing in France. Why hadn't the others visited her? Concerned themselves about her? Elizabeth and Sophia frequently visited the Continent. Poor Sophia. She and Mama were together now, all misunderstandings cleared away.

He managed to decipher a few more words.

For many years . . . adorned the stage . . . her comic wit . . . sweetness of her voice . . . second to none . . . her generosity and kindness of heart . . . relieving the necessitous.

Annos 50
July 5th 1816.
Mementote Lugete
(Remember and weep for her)

That was all any of them could now do. Remember and weep for her. The tears were coursing down his cheeks. It was a shameful thought that this headstone had been placed there, not by his father, not by any of her children, but by theatrical friends, Mr. and Mrs. Henry Woodgate. Shameful, too, that her few private possessions had to be sold by public auction to meet her debts. Most shameful of all was that the funeral expenses had not been settled until three years later.

Slowly he retraced his steps to the waiting carriage. He must not miss the train to Calais. These newfangled trains were certainly marvelous for covering the miles, and as for the steamships . . . why, crossing the Channel was no longer a penance.

It was George Cambridge who brought the news. Adelaide's eyes had lit up with pleasure when he was announced, but the next moment she was asking, "What is it, George? What has happened?"

Several times he began, and each time failed, but finally managed, "It's the Earl of Munster . . ."

"George Fitzclarence? He's ill? No . . . he's . . ."

"Dead, dear Aunt Adelaide." He put a comforting arm around her as she asked tremulously, "How?"

"He . . . he . . . shot himself . . ."

For what seemed an endless time she did not speak. Then in a whisper:

"Suicide . . . is such grievous sin. But vy? Vy? He had everything to live for. Vealth . . . position . . ."

"His doctors are already saying that his mind was disturbed . . ."

"Pray God that vill be the verdict, so that he may have a Christian burial . . . Do you know, George, he vas the first to greet me on my arrival in England . . . just a shy young boy, but not too shy to tell me of his love for a lady . . ."

"Minney Seymour. Yes, he loved her since they played together as children, but it was an unrequited love."

Silence fell between them, George deeming it wiser to give his aunt time to get over the shock. Outside, the blustery March wind was bending and swaying the trees, but in Adelaide's room, all was warmth and comfort. Warmth and comfort; comfort of home, warmth of a woman's love. Why shouldn't they be his? His aunt's voice broke in on his thoughts. "George . . . haven't you anything else to tell me?"

"To tell you, dear Aunt? Such as?"

"Since the Queen's marriage, I have noticed an ever-increasing . . . how shall I say it . . . joyousness about you. At first I thought it vas because your parents and sisters had come to live here in London, and then I began to realize it vas a different kind of happiness . . . and I vaited . . . hoping you vould tell me. Since then I have heard rumors . . . ugly rumors . . ."

"No, Aunt Adelaide. Nothing ugly. On the contrary, very, very beautiful . . ."

"Then tell me, George."

"You know it concerns a lady . . . and I love her very much . . . just in the way I always knew I should love her when we met . . ."

"But she is not royal . . ."

"No, Ma'am, no. But why should that make any difference?"

"Oh, George, George. Has all my teaching been in vain? Is it true then that the Queen has refused permission for your marriage?"

"Only too true, dear Aunt, but I shall marry her despite my cousin's vindictiveness."

"But she vill not be able to go to court. Any children born to you vill not be able to succeed . . . Think again, dear George . . ."

"It is too late, Aunt Adelaide. I have given my heart. We are already living as man and wife . . ." He went over to her chair, kneeling by her side. "Never, never did I think I should know such wonderful joy. There will never be any regrets, never any talk of sacrifice . . ."

"But an actress, George . . ."

"I am not the first prince to love an actress, and she, like one other we both know of, is most worthy . . . most lovable . . ."

The tone of his voice—his bluntness—roused her. "Somevhere . . . somehow . . . I have failed both of you and your parents. First you refused to be considered as the Queen's consort—now you take an actress as your mistress." Then her voice softened . . . "but I do vish you happiness, George."

He kissed her. "Thank you, dear Aunt Adelaide. May I bring my dearest Louise to call on you . . . to get your blessing?"

She smiled sadly, suddenly remembering that the other George, George Fitzclarence would never call again. "You know, dear boy, how I love having guests and callers."

The Hon. Mrs. Minney Dawson-Damer had inherited many of Mrs. Fitzherbert's traits, one being able to extract the utmost out of any social occasion. She had now been married for seventeen years; she was the mother of three daughters and a son, but she was still enthusiastic about this her forty-fourth birthday.

Carrying on her good training, her daughters had

prepared a "birthday table" for her, and when they met for breakfast no one was more excited than Minney.

The children were well aware of what each was giving dear Mama but were most intrigued to see the presents from Papa and Aunt Maryanne, not forgetting all the other mysterious parcels from friends piled on another table.

Minney opened each parcel with appropriate exclamations of surprise and thanks, and then moved over to the other table. What could be in that carefully wrapped, securely tied box? The handwriting was distinctly foreign. She appealed to her husband that he should cut the cord.

Everyone watched breathlessly as paper was removed, then packing of shavings, until a final covering of red velvet was lifted, revealing the most beautiful of mantel-time-pieces. It was her husband who picked up the visiting card.

"Who . . . who sent it? It must have cost . . ."

For answer, he gently placed her in a chair, before showing her the card.

"George Fitzclarence! But he's . . . ! Oh no, no. He must have bought this before . . . before . . ."

"Exactly, my dear. He must have bought it in Paris before returning home to shoot himself, after arranging for its delivery on this your birthday."

"Poor, poor George. Look at these forget-me-nots. And these sprigs of rosemary. Rosemary for remembrance." She sighed. "I don't think I can eat any breakfast."

Sixteen-year-old daughter Minney was examining the clock. "How he must have loved you, Mama. To have been faithful to you all these years . . . to have thought of you in his last hours . . ."

"That's enough, Miss. Get on with your breakfast. I am going back to my room," and picking up the clock, left her family discussing Mama's late lamented admirer.

She had never wept for George Fitzclarence. She had felt annoyance when he had pursued her with his protestations of love; she had felt pity when he ended his own life; now, for the first time, she felt remorse, only now realizing the hurt her rebuffs must have caused.

As *Sudbury House* had been the scene of her almost-fatal illness, the doctors ordered that she must look elsewhere for a winter retreat. With Ida as companion and adviser, she decided to make a round of visits to various country mansions that had been placed at her disposal. The medical gentlemen held up their hands in horror. The traveling entailed might be fatal! Adelaide laughed at their fears. What about these new railway trains? Why shouldn't she use them? True, the Duke of Wellington was strongly opposed to them saying they would encourage the lower orders to "move about," but there was no denying their speed.

Like two excited young misses, Adelaide and Ida traveled from the London Rail terminus to Southampton in less than three hours. From there they crossed over to the Isle of Wight, found nowhere to their liking, so returned and toured Dorset, finally settling on *Canford House*.

September found her in residence, with, as usual, Lord Howe and his daughter in attendance. Whether she was entertaining, or being entertained; whether they were having a quiet dinner at home . . . riding . . . driving . . . Richard Howe was never far from her side. She knew that people talked; that they speculated as to the outcome; she a widow . . . he a widower. Only in the quiet of the night, when sleep eluded her, did she let her mind center round the question. He would have to declare his love before she could mention marriage . . . for, being royal, the actual proposal would have to come from her. What had she to offer him? A frail, sick woman with only a few more years to live. There were times, she was sure, when his consideration and devotion spoke of love, yet she dare not bring herself to speak, lest she should disrupt their existing happiness, content that they were together.

The villagers quickly fell under her spell; for along with her household she helped in every good work, and gave liberally to all the charities. No one in the village that winter went short of food, clothing or coal. More children were persuaded to attend school despite Lord Melbourne, the Prime Minister, being against education for the poor, saying the children would be of greater assistance to their parents if they went into the factories.

She was back at *Marlborough House* in time for the wedding of her niece, Princess Augusta of Cambridge. With her romantic yearnings she still adored attending weddings, but when the day arrived, she was so ill that she was unable to have the pleasure of seeing the bride wearing the diamond tiara and necklace that had been her gift. As soon as she was on her feet, she returned to *Bushey*.

Despite almost overwhelming weariness, riding was still her favorite pleasure. Richard Howe guarded her carefully; determining the speed of her mount, and the distance.

Those were the moments she enjoyed; when they were alone, free to talk easily without eavesdroppers picking up odd remarks and magnifying them.

It was during one of these outings, their horses almost at walking-pace, that Richard broached the subject so uppermost in her mind.

"Would you, Ma'am, think it advisable that I should remarry? I mean, Ma'am, with my large family of ten children, do you think any lady would take on the task?"

She had hesitated, but only for a moment.

"If the lady has any true affection for you, Sir, why not?"

"The only way, then, Ma'am, is to plead my case. Perhaps, Ma'am, you could help me. If you could speak to the lady . . . mention my admiration . . ."

"The lady?" The words came unbidden, in the shock of realization . . . realization that he was not referring to her.

"Yes, Miss Anne Gore. You know her well, her mother being one of your ladies-in-waiting. She is, as you know, of mature age . . . fond of children . . ."

She let him go on singing the praises of Anne Gore.

It was all over now. What little time was left to her . . . she must go on alone . . . and who could blame Richard?

She essayed a smile. "You have chosen vell, Richard. I am indeed fond of Anne, and will certainly speak with her. Just think! Another vedding for me to attend! You know how partial I am to veddings."

Yet that night, when her dresser had drawn the curtains of the bed and left the room, she wept for the shattering of a dream . . . a dream whose only substance was a loyal courtier's devotion.

Country house after country house; always in search of the air that would restore her to health, until the doctors in despair suggested that she should go to Madeira. She played for time. Perhaps, but in the meantime she would spend the summer at *Bushey*.

It was there that they brought the news of the death of Minney Seymour. It seemed incredible . . . she was so young. Then she recalled that Minney's parents, Lord Hugh and Lady Horatio Seymour, had both died of the wasting disease. Why was it that doctors could not find a cure? Other men of science were finding methods to make the railway engines travel faster and faster, having now reached a speed of thirty miles an hour. Surely the study of this killer disease was of more importance than this craze for speed.

The visit to Madeira was on a grand scale, taking a household staff of thirty-six, in addition to her personal attendants. Her sister was in the party . . . and of course Lord and Lady Howe . . . and their recently born son, of whom naturally, Adelaide was godmother!

She reveled in the sunshine . . . walking . . . still occasionally riding, and visiting the fisherfolk, winning their affection for her liberality.

Still the cough and rheumatism persisted and when she returned in April, she felt that she had made her last sea voyage. Whatever time was left to her, she would spend it in England.

The joy of returning home was immediately dashed by

the news that Princess Sophia was at the point of death. Without hesitation, Adelaide hastened to her side and was with her to the end. Hardly had she been laid to rest, when came more shattering news that Maryanne Smith, the Hon. Mrs. Jerningham, the second adopted daughter of Mrs. Fitzherbert, had also died at the early age of forty-six.

Adelaide's heart went out to the widower and motherless children. Why, why, oh why did such tragedies have to happen?

Bemused and bewildered she felt herself floundering in a welter of grief and tears, but bravely pulled herself together to be godmother once again. In a cream lace gown, her diamonds sparkling, she held Victoria's newest baby, Princess Louise; her dormant mother-love awakening and shining in her eyes.

During her absence, the doctors had decided on *Bentley Priory,* near Watford, as her winter residence. There she had two rooms on the ground floor for her bedroom and boudoir, and as they led into a conservatory, she was able to sit beneath palms on the coldest of English days, pretending she was back in Madeira.

When she visited *Bushey* the villagers looked one at another in askance. They had never before seen her looking so ill, and when in September, she said goodbye prior to returning to *Bentley Priory,* they knew that next Christmas there would be no joints of beef nor bags of coal for them.

Epilogue

She felt very comfortable and rested. Of course it was the opiates that they were giving her; she must have rest, to regain her strength. It would soon be Christmas. Would she be well enough to give her usual children's parties? Of course they were not on the scale of those Pavilion parties . . . those were wonderful affairs. She could see them all now; little boys and girls dashing in and out between the white-painted tables looking for their names. What joy it had been buying and choosing the toys! The vision of Mina Kennedy-Erskine rose before her; standing, hands behind her back, watching Jemmet wash her grandfather's hair. Dear little Mina. She found herself wondering if William knew about Mina . . . knew that his favorite grand-daughter, born on the day of his accession, was now married to George, second Earl of Munster, his eldest grandson.

She had been a radiant bride. No arranged marriage here. True, romantic love, such as she had dreamt of. Please God, they would have greater happiness than the first earl and his wife, but there were no golden rules as to how happiness could be achieved. Mina would have to face up to life and learn how to extract the sweet from the bitter, even as she had done.

George Cambridge, too, had found that priceless possession but he had had to pay a big price for his love; a morganatic marriage, unacknowledged both by the Queen and his parents, refusing to meet his beloved Louisa.

She, however, had been more daring, repeatedly entertaining him and his wife, together with their three boys, but the dignity of royalty must be upheld, and the meetings were kept secret.

It was getting dark now. Why didn't they bring in the lamps? She was glad they still had lamps at *Bentley Priory*. She didn't like the new horrid smelly gaslighting.

She put out her hand, and immediately felt the comforting pressure of Ida's. Dear Ida . . . No one had ever had a more loving sister. Trying to remember, everything seemed to have begun on Ida's wedding day . . . her own marriage . . . and all those other brides . . . they were crowding in on her . . . all lifting their faces to be kissed . . . to be wished happiness . . . all so ethereal looking in their white satin and lace, and pearls and diamonds . . . hundreds and hundreds of them.

When her little daughter, Elizabeth, had died, Ida understood the anguish and sent little crippled Louise and Prince Edward, to give what comfort they could to their aunt, and she had gratefully accepted their love. Why had God denied her a child? Soon, my little *liebchen* . . . I shall hold you in my arms again . . . never to let you go.

Was it yesterday that Victoria and Albert had visited her, giving all the news about the children? Pussy and Bertie were becoming quite grown up, driving around in the barouche that she had given them. How many more were in the royal nursery? She tried hard to remember, but failed, except to recall that another was on the way. Would she again be asked to be a godmother?

The Duchess of Kent was a frequent visitor, mixing her prayers with her recounting of Victoria's shortcomings. How she and William had detested each other, but it didn't matter now. Nothing mattered. Everything was arranged. She had made her will and left full instructions.

There were the five betrothal rings William had sent her; one for each Fitzclarence girl, and Frederick's wife to have that which should have been Sophia's. Then the lovely diamond bracelet, William's last gift. That was for the Duchess of Gloucester. For the Fitzclarence boys there were the family portraits, including several of their mother, long kept in the *Bushey* attics, all save but one which still held pride of place in the drawing-room.

She had tried to remember everyone . . . there were so many dear friends . . . so many grandchildren . . . gifts for all of them . . . for dear Richard Howe . . . and his wife . . .

Ida felt Adelaide's hold on her hand slacken. She called to the nurse. Adelaide, with a smile on her face, had gone to join her loved ones.

She had wanted no procession, but nevertheless a Guard of Honor escorted her from *Bentley Priory* to Windsor; their red coats giving a splash of color to the grey December day. All the villagers along the route came out to see her pass, remembering her generosity and kindness, while the mournful dirge of the church bells tolled her passing.

Before the hearse, came Adelaide's own carriage, occupied by her equerry, Captain Taylor, carrying her crown, the one she had had made from her own jewels.

Further along the route, the Prince Consort, with four of Victoria's carriages, joined the procession, which on arriving at Windsor was received by the Duke and Duchess of Cambridge, Prince George, the Duchess of Kent and the Duchess of Weimar.

In accordance with her wish, ten sailors carried the coffin into St. George's Chapel with Frederick and Adolphus Fitzclarence walking on either side.

There were no scintillating uniforms of foreign rulers or ambassadors . . . not even a sprinkling of cabinet ministers; just her chaplains and doctors, her maids and her pages . . . and Lord Howe.

Sorrowfully he watched the coffin being lowered to rest beside that of her husband and baby daughter. He had done his utmost to serve her; at first pitying her in her difficult rôle; then admiring her for her courage, till finally, loving her as the truly noble, lovable woman that she was.

Silently he knelt down by the open grave. The crack, as he broke his wand of office, shattered the silence of the chapel; a salute to the passing of Adelaide, consort of William IV.